Library
Brevard Junior College
Cocoa, Florida

THE BAKER'S CART
AND OTHER TALES

THE BAKER'S CART
and other tales

by GERALD WILLIAM BULLETT
(1894-1958)

Short Story Index Reprint Series

 BOOKS FOR LIBRARIES PRESS
FREEPORT, NEW YORK

First Published 1926
Reprinted 1970

STANDARD BOOK NUMBER:
8369-3575-6

LIBRARY OF CONGRESS CATALOG CARD NUMBER:
77-125208

PRINTED IN THE UNITED STATES OF AMERICA

To
J. B. PRIESTLEY

CONTENTS

	PAGE
THE BAKER'S CART	1
SIMPSON'S FUNERAL	19
THE BENDING SICKLE	37
ATTITUDES	59
MRS PUSEY'S CHICKENS	77
THE RENEWAL OF YOUTH	97
SUMMERS END	117
LAST DAYS OF BINNACLE	143
THREE SUNDAYS	175
THE SUNFLOWERS	195
QUEER'S RIVAL	221
THE DARK HOUSE	241
PRENTICE	287

THE BAKER'S CART

THE BAKER'S CART

FATHER was again in disgrace. Mother was once more beet-red with indignation. 'My dear!' cried he in bewilderment . . . but even that was turned against him. If only he'd *dear* less and *do* more! Mother was as skilful in debate as in housekeeping: waste was abhorrent to her, whether of words or of halfpennies. Her habit in controversy was to stab out with one phrase, and then remain silent for a period of days. Father, divining that such a period was about to begin, lost no time in venting his anger, not upon the cause of it, but upon nine-year-old Harriet bending in terror over her porridge, upon the green venetian blinds, the wallpaper, the *Pears' Annual* pictures, and all the appurtenances of the breakfast room in which they sat, husband, wife, and youngest daughter. He declared that the wallpaper was poisonous, that the pictures were hung crooked, and that the architect who planned french windows to open on a backyard littered with drains was an imbecile.

'Take your hair out of your plate, Harriet,' he said, in parenthesis.

The ghost of a smile played and passed over the face of Mother, a smile which Harriet interpreted as full and free forgiveness of Father's reference to the wallpaper of her choice, and to the pictures her hands had hung. For Mother was always thinking of others, self-abnegation being the most conspicuous of her virtues. Harriet expected her every moment to say to the culprit, as she had so often said to her children : 'It is not of me you must ask pardon, but of Him above.'

At the moment Father seemed disinclined to ask pardon of any one. He continued his indictment of Number 27, Coniston Villas, and extended its application until the whole universe appeared clouded with his displeasure. He enquired, with some bitterness, why Alice and Maud were not at breakfast. Incredible blunder ; for Alice and Maud, those hard-worked elder sisters of Harriet, had broken their fast and hurried away to their dingy city offices fully fifteen minutes before he, their erring father, had emerged from his so-called workroom. It was not often *they* had a Saturday off, oh no ! Mother could not forbear to break her strategic silence with this information.

The storm of Father's angry eloquence rose and fell and rose again, until, presently, he seemed to gulp it back. He pushed away his plate with such violence that the bacon fat he had left upon it became a turbulent sea, whose waves washed forward to the table-cloth and backward to the pushing fingers. Whereat he muttered an unknown word, wiped the offended finger on his napkin, and loped out of the room like an awkward schoolboy.

Mother heaved a deep sigh. She rose from the table with infinite dignity and, from the greater height, shot one keen, wistful glance at her daughter's bowed head. Harriet, though she kept her eyes averted, was conscious of that glance, which she knew to be a sign that Mother's cross was almost more than she could bear, and that Mother's little girl must comfort Mother by being very good and sweet and helpful, particularly in respect of the dirty breakfast things. But Harriet chose to ignore the appeal. She allowed Mother unaided to pile up the plates and gather together the knives and forks; and when, a few minutes later, Mother returned from the kitchen with a tray, Harriet was lying on her back under the table. The defection cost her a pang. She knew that, given the opportunity, Mother would pet and praise her, and say what a blessing she was. It was very nice to be a blessing ; and Mother was so dear and adorable, with her lovely olive skin and her eyes of tenderness, that she could not be resisted. Harriet, on the few occasions that she had tried to resist, had always finally surrendered with tears and contrite kisses : it was as though Mother, by the very abundance of her love, levied tribute on this miraculous child of her middle-age. What could Harriet do but love the mother to whom she owed so much, the mother who fed and clothed her, played with her, told her stories, and slaved, for her sake and her sisters', to keep the home together ? ' We'll have no secrets from each other, will we, Babs dear ! I want to know everything, *everything*, that goes on in that funny little brown head of yours.' Mother loved her voraciously, and wished not to share her, even with Alice and Maud, still less with Father, whose mysterious wickedness it was—violent temper, lack of ambition, love of idle hobbies and unproductive dreaming—that threatened the home with disruption. Harriet feared her father almost as much as she loved her mother. She hated him sometimes, on her mother's behalf, for his unkindness. Yet even in the love she owed, and diligently paid, to her mother, there was a lurking and unrecognised fear. Something deep within her shrank from the ultimate surrender, something struggled against being absorbed into that other and so powerful personality. In spite of the maternal edict, Harriet did withhold secrets : trivial, childish things, thoughts and hopes of less than gossamer substance ; yet they were precious to her, the more so because they were intimately, inviolably, her very own. 'You're such a nice baby, I could gobble you up,' cried Mother in her raptures ; 'all your youth and freshness. They make *me* a child again, you little mousie ! ' And though it was great fun to be gobbled up with kisses, Harriet contrived to withhold her innermost treasure from the insatiable heart that laid siege to it.

Under the table she lay at peace, fancying herself a princess, the four table-legs the posts of a great, royal bed, and the underside of the table the dim purple canopy. Then she began playing the most secret and delicious of all her games, which she called Going Inside. Inside was her peculiar paradise. It was tingling, glowing, a riot of lovely colours in perpetual motion. It was a little wood where squirrels sat nibbling nuts on the green banks of a stream that trickled, with jewel clarity, over a pebbly bed ; a region where, beyond time and space, the eternal fairy-tales mingled in spontaneous fantasy. It was fragrant to the nostrils, comforting to the palate, a refuge for the mind. It smelt of honeysuckle and pines and moist earth ; it tasted like a precious stone. And Mother had never been there.

From this country of the mind, after a few moments, Harriet was dragged back, abruptly, to a consideration of her father and his misdeeds ; and as she pondered the mystery an adventurous impulse moved in her. Father was now, she guessed, in that little shed at the bottom of the garden which he called, to Mother's disgust, his workroom : the place where, in idle moments, he carved and chipped and carpentered to his heart's content. She did not love Father, because he did not deserve to be loved ; but to-day the mystery of his personality excited her a little. She resolved, with a sudden intake of the breath, to visit the baffling creature in its own iniquitous den.

2

Father was at work with a long, flexible saw. He was red in the face, and emitting little grunts of exertion. Sometimes the saw, having reached the end of its outgoing journey, refused to be pulled back, and then the tapering end seemed like a ripple of steel-grey water. Father paused, mopped his brow, and flung a surprised glance at Harriet, who stood shyly in the doorway.

'Well, and what are you after?' His tone was uninviting.

Harriet hung her head. 'I don't know.'

'Did your mother send you with a message?'

'No,' said Harriet. 'I just wanted to see . . . Oh, Father, what a lovely workhouse you've got!"

Father permitted himself to grin. 'You've seen it often enough before, haven't you?'

'I haven't *really*, you know,' explained Harriet. 'I've just sort of looked a tiny peep; that's all.'

'You're sure your mother didn't send you?' said Father, suspicion reappearing in his eye.

'Trufa-nonna!' declared Harriet, earnestly. 'I just thought I'd look you up, don't you see.'

Father laughed. 'You're a rum child. Want to see what's going on, eh?'

Harriet nodded. 'What are you making, Father?'

'Making nothing at present. Sawing up

planks for use later on. But I made something this morning. Like to see it?'

'Yes, please,' answered Harriet, dissembling her delight.

'But it's a secret, mind!'

It didn't seem to matter, after all, that she did not love Father. This warm comfortable feeling inside her was so much better than love. Here was Father, that bad man, about to tell her a secret. That was a thing that Mother had never done. Mother extracted confidences, but never gave them. This was different, this new experience, and much more exciting. Father, knowing nothing of commerce, was unbosoming himself without demanding anything. Harriet was enchanted by his curtness, his casualness, his man-to-man air.

'It's a little thing I've invented,' said Father, with engaging vanity. 'A mangle, you see. You clamp it down to the kitchen table with these two screws; and this roller travels over the board and back again, squeezing the clothes dry. See? All you have to do is to turn this handle.'

'Oo!' cried Harriet. And she added, with her most ladylike and adult air: 'Did you make it all this morning, every teeny bit of it?'

'Well, no,' admitted the inventor. 'Not exactly all. I had the roller done yesterday, and the board partly done. But I ribbed the board this morning, and fitted the whole thing together. Got up three hours earlier so's to get it done before breakfast. It was to be a surprise, don't you see.'

Magic phrase! 'A surprise. Who for? For Mother?'

Father shrugged his shoulders. 'It's here when she wants it.'

Harriet understood; but she remained silent, nodding wisely.

'I suppose,' she ventured, 'you couldn't make something for me, could you? You haven't time, I expect.'

Father's queer smile gave her courage to be more explicit.

'I do so want something. It isn't a very big thing.'

'Well, what is it?' demanded Father, gruffly, becoming very busy with the saw once more.

'Only a baker's cart,' pleaded Harriet. 'Is it very hard to make a baker's cart?'

'Baker's cart!' said Father, with unashamed conceit. 'Easiest thing in the world, a baker's cart is. You watch, my dear!'

He strode over to his scrap-heap, hovered for a moment in contemplation, and then pounced on some pieces of wood. 'Now, here we are. Let's get to work with the fret-saw.' He got to work with the fret-saw, and with a hammer and tiny tintacks. 'There you are—there's the beginning of your cart! Nice high cart bakers live in, with big yellow wheels, or do you prefer green wheels?'

'Red wheels,' said Harriet.

'Red as blood,' agreed Father, in his excitement. 'And now we'll make a partition here, and a dropboard fastened up with hooks and eyes like all the best dropboards. . . . Now that little place is where the loaves go, see.'

'Oo, the loaves!'

'Quite so. *Oo, the loaves,* is what the baker calls out; at least, ours does. He calls out just as he jumps off the step of his cart. Now, where shall we find something for a step? Two steps, in fact. One each side.'

'And wheels? What are we going to make the wheels of?'

But Father had already cut out two circular discs of thin wood.

'But they must have spikes!' objected Harriet.

'A very fair criticism,' admitted Father. 'Spokes they shall have. We arrive at spokes by a process of elimination. Thus!' He sketched out the spokes with his stump of fat pencil—that fascinating pencil!—and again set to work with the fret-saw.

Harriet began to dance up and down, clapping her hands, as the baker's cart took shape before her eyes. Her slim, black-stockinged legs twinkled as she darted to and fro amid the litter of carpentry. These outbursts were rare: lyrical and irrepressible. For the most part she stood in speechless rapture, large eyes shining with joy from her peaked, elfish face.

'After lunch, a coat of paint,' said Father, gazing at his creation with pardonable satisfaction.

3

Mother stood in the doorway of the shed. She was displeased.

'Harriet! I've been looking for you everywhere. What are you doing here, hindering your father in his work?'

'Only just watching, Mother.'

'Well, run along now and get your things on. I'm going to visit the Cottage Hospital. There's just time before lunch. You'd like to come with me, wouldn't you, darling?'

'Yes,' said Harriet, without enthusiasm.

On the way into the house Mother asked: 'What is that new toy you've got there, dear? Show Mother.'

Harriet's fist reluctantly yielded up its treasure. 'A baker's cart.'

'A baker's cart. Aren't you getting a little too old for bakers' carts, Harriet? Where did you get it?'

'Father made it for me.'

'Indeed!' Mother's tone was chillier than ever. 'Be quick and get your boots buttoned up, my child.'

On the way to the Cottage Hospital, to which every few weeks it was Mother's habit to take a basket of bounty, she talked to Harriet about the duty of kindness to those less fortunately circumstanced than ourselves. 'We're going to see those poor little orphans, Harriet. You remember?'

Harriet remembered.

'Just a few dainties I'm taking them,' said Mother, blithely. 'It will give them so much pleasure, poor dears!'

Harriet agreed, her eyes moistening.

'Now isn't there any little thing you'd like to give?' said Mother, persuasively.

THE BAKER'S CART

'There's poor Tommy Fish, who had that dreadful operation and will never be able to walk again. Think what that means, Harriet.'

Harriet, clutching her mother's hand, trotted along in dumb distress.

'It would be nice to brighten the little fellow's life, wouldn't it, dear, if only for a day or two?'

'Oh, Mother,' said Harriet. 'Shall I go back and fetch my Noah's Ark. I'm too old for that now, aren't I?'

'Yes, dear. But it's not very kind to give away only the things we don't want ourselves, is it?'

Harriet grew red with shame. 'What shall I give him, Mother?'

'I don't want to influence you,' said Mother. 'It is for you to decide. A real sacrifice. If you feel you can. Now, if I were you . . . there's this pretty little baker's cart.'

'But that's at home,' said Harriet, quickly.

Mother produced the baker's cart from her muff. 'No, dear. Here it is.'

'Oh, dear, he can't have that! He shan't!'

'A poor little orphan, Harriet,'

Harriet whimpered. 'I want it myself. I do. I've wanted it a long time. I don't believe Him above will mind me keeping it. I've got so many other things that I wouldn't miss. And Tommy Fish 'd like them just as well.'

'It's not only Tommy I'm thinking of, darling. It's you too. It is more blessed to give, you know. . . . But, of course, I shan't force you.'

Resentment, anger, fear, and despair: these in turn were Harriet's dominant emotions as they finished their walk to the Cottage Hospital. Admitted to the convalescent ward, Mother distributed her gifts, going from bed to bed like an angel of mercy. Finally she paused at the foot of a bed where a pale-faced urchin lay stretched on his back grinning gallantly whenever a visitor addressed him.

'Here's Tommy Fish,' said Mother. 'How are you this morning, Tommy?'

Tommy's boast of being much better this morning was cut short by a twinge of pain.

Harriet's lip quivered. She turned away her face and nudged her mother. 'Give it to him, please, Mother.'

'Are you quite sure——' began Mother,

'Yes. I want him to have it.' A moment ago Harriet had hated Tommy Fish. But now she burned with hatred for something else, she knew not what, some shadowy thing that had made irony of the boy's cheerful answer.

'Tommy, my Harriet has brought you something. Just a little toy.'

Harriet hid her flaming face during this ceremony. She wanted nothing but release from this house of torment. She tugged at her mother's arm.

To step into the open air again was like waking from an evil dream. Mother was still talkative, though subdued. As they entered the house she asked: 'Are you glad, dear, or sorry that you parted with your little cart?'

'Glad,' whispered Harriet.

'That's right.' Harriet's mother was moved, perhaps by compunction. Her voice trembled a little.

'Tommy Fish is an orphan, isn't he, Mother? That means he hasn't got a father, doesn't it?'

'Yes, dear. No mother or father.'

'Oh,' cried Harriet, 'I'm so glad he had my baker's cart. 'Cause I've still got Father, haven't I?'

Mother's face flamed, and paled as swiftly. She clenched her hands, and her eyes faltered as they strove to meet the innocent gaze of Harriet. She knew herself defeated.

SIMPSON'S FUNERAL

SIMPSON'S FUNERAL

THEY came from the four points of the compass to Simpson's funeral; yet when all the guests were assembled they numbered no more than fifteen. A scattered family, but a faithful one nevertheless. They had spread a fine network of correspondence, like a spider's web, all over England. The hundred small jealousies, the rankling memories, and the necessity for taking sides in the great subterranean quarrel between Simpson and his wife: these had seldom or never been allowed to ripple the surface of that correspondence, still less to stop it. Whatever happened, little George's operation for rupture must be reported to his grandfather; however derelict from his own duties, Lucy's uncle must be invited to share the general disapprobation of Lucy's engagement to a penniless Channel Islander of unknown antecedents. As grandfather, as uncle, Simpson had been an unqualified success. 'Very likely,' his daughters would say. 'You don't have to live with him, my dears,'

The house was in a state of quiet, mournful, important bustle. Aunt Elizabeth, clutching a little wad of pocket-handkerchief, tiptoed into the room where lilies shed their ghastly pallor and their sickly perfume. She stepped with an exaggerated care, closing the door softly, as if in fear of waking her dead brother. A mean little room with a florid wallpaper and crowded with heavy furniture : an old walnut piano, a mahogany table pushed into a corner to make room for the coffin, a bookcase full of unread Victorian classics, a sofa shrouded in a dustsheet. A large gilt ormolu clock stood on the mantelpiece, flanked by family photographs and lustreware. Curtains draped the french windows, and a thick gloom, compounded of scent and dusk and summer heat, pervaded the room like a personal presence. Everything here was mere lumber now, including Simpson himself. Elizabeth recoiled from the thought even in the moment of entertaining it. The dim atmosphere pressed cold fingers upon her mind ; the slow ticking of the clock—a clock he had always hated—tapped into her heart a message of complete indifference. While she stood, looking and listening, that ticking came to an abrupt end, leaving the room in the possession of a silence that was more than Elizabeth could endure. In that moment of paralysis, that nightmare of atrophied volition, she stood in an eternal tomb, all existence seeming to her tortured fancy no more than a tale of deaths. First one, then another ; and no knowing on whom next the doom would fall. First her child, then her husband, and now her favourite brother. Shivering, as with mortal cold, she turned back to the door. ' Everything in perfect taste,' said her lips dutifully ; and they repeated the phrase to her niece, Edith Simpson, who awaited her in the corridor. ' Such nice flowers, my dear,' added Aunt Elizabeth, bravely resuming her necessary role.

Edith nodded, and kissed the older woman's cheek. With a little encouragement she would have burst into tears once again. She was preoccupied with grief, and felt it right that she should be so preoccupied. Somewhere at the back of her mind was the conviction that never for one moment must she forget that her father was dead, her mother broken-hearted, and herself left burdened with sorrow and untold responsibility. It troubled her secretly that thoughts of this and that would sometimes intrude to seduce her from this undeviating fidelity. There were so many things to be done, arrangements to be made, people to be written to, condolences to be acknowledged ; but she herself had held aloof from these tedious distractions. They would have provided a relief of sorts, forgetfulness ; and that was the last thing she desired. All her mind and soul must be concentrated upon the dark task of mourning : that was her debt, and she would pay it in full. Anything else, anything more active, would have been less than right and proper. Luckily there was Rose, her youngest and only married sister, to help see after things. On Rose Burnett's young shoulders rested the conduct of nearly all these merely practical affairs. She had come, in response to a telegram, bringing with her (since he could not be left at home untended) her three-year-old son ; and, promptly upon her appearance, Mrs Simpson had retired to nurse her grief and her grievance in sensational solitude, and Edith had given herself up to the feeding of that emotion with periodic visits. Thankful as she was for Rose's capable domestic management, she could not stifle the reproachful feeling that there was something a little callous in such efficiency. But Rose, of course, having a husband and a child, could not be expected to cower under the blow as did those to whom poor Father had been everything, everything.

Extraordinary, nevertheless, how selfish marriage had made her.

Edith loved Aunt Elizabeth because Aunt Elizabeth was a member of the family, her father's sister ; and family sentiment so far triumphed over the natural antipathy that divided the two women as to impel them, for a brief moment, into each other's arms. Edith kissed her aunt with mournful emphasis, receiving in return a peck and a pat on the shoulder that were altogether too brisk, she thought, for such an occasion. Elizabeth was in fact a little disconcerted by the embrace, which she divined to be more ritualistic than affectionate. She disengaged herself, murmuring 'Cheer up, my dear,' and walked unsteadily down the corridor that led to the room where the other guests were collected. She overtook Rose.

'Where's Master Dickie ? ' she asked, with an attempt at mild gaiety.

'In the garden, I think,' Rose answered, 'talking to Uncle Harry. . . . Has everybody arrived ? '

'All except Uncle Tom. It isn't like him to be late. What can have happened ? '

Rose shrugged her shoulders, which was the nearest she ever permitted herself to a shudder. 'Oh, don't talk about things happening ! He was written to, right enough.'

Rose wrinkled her brow, giving, in that moment, a hint of what she would look like at thirty-five. Small, brown, comely, she seemed to Elizabeth a gallant, pathetic figure, prematurely burdened with the responsibilities of middle age. 'Written to, and telephoned. Telephoned at once.'

'Of course,' nodded Aunt Elizabeth. 'He's the executor, I suppose. Being unpunctual is one of his professional tricks, no doubt.' She spoke good-humouredly, as if bantering the absent brother.

They joined the rest of the family, who were in the morning room, pulling on new black gloves, staring gloomily out of the window, or fidgeting with this or that part of their attire. All were self-conscious and miserable, wishing the hateful business over. The only man among them who seemed to be, even for a moment, unaware of his surroundings was Edward Simpson, the youngest of the dead man's brothers. He was absorbed in his own thoughts, from which no parade of horror seemed able to distract him. He was wishing he had kept in closer touch with poor old Fred. There had never been anything but good-feeling between the two, but they had drifted apart, circumstances aiding, and Edward had been at no pains to arrest the drift.

For that he now blamed himself bitterly. Fred had not prospered, either in love or in business, as he, Edward, had prospered. His marriage had not been an unqualified success, nor had it been that next-best thing, a complete and recognised failure. So much Edward surmised, and had surmised long ago. Sitting now, in the house of mourning, tapping with his fingers on the arms of his chair, and absently scrutinising his boots, pictures of the past pressed upon him bringing with them stabbing intimations of a sympathy, a brotherly bond, that might have been and now could never be. Sometimes, once or twice a year perhaps, the two men had met in the city, where business took them both every week-day of their lives, and lunched together, exchanging polite gossip. Edward remembered vividly the last of such occasions, remembered, with a fresh and poignant emotion, how old, how *tired*, his brother had looked. The grey-white hair and the lined features were those of a man prematurely aged at sixty, but the eyes, though infinitely weary, held still a hint of the pathetic eagerness of youth. They were the eyes of a boy, eyes sick with disappointment, yet still timid, in fugitive moments, with a kind of hurt surprise, a wistfulness. Well, he would never look like that again. Whatever his troubles had been, they were over now. . . . But the trite reflection did but add fuel to the fire of Edward's brooding contrition. Suddenly he was overwhelmed by an invasion of earlier, more cruel memories : he was once more the little brother, and Fred, magnificent from boarding school, was giving him the cigarette pictures he had deigned to collect during the term for him. Edward's hands leaped to his face to shut him in with his memories. Then he became aware that he was in a roomful of people, and he stiffened. 'Uncle Tom not come yet, Rose?' he enquired briskly.

They all, the women in particular, felt some compunction about setting off without Tom, the dead man's eldest brother. Even Elizabeth, his senior by six years, felt that she hardly dared acquiesce in the disposal of these mortal remains until the masterful head of the house had admitted the sad necessity. Perhaps she nursed the foolish fancy that brother Tom, known among his acquaintances as a man not to be trifled with, could bluster even Death himself into surrender. But the funeral could not be delayed indefinitely : both for obvious reasons and because human nerves could not stand a prolongation of the ordeal, the decisive step must be taken. Everything was ready. The mourners filed into the dingy hall, and down the gravel path ; with ill-concealed eagerness to be done with it all they scrambled into the waiting carriages. Rose remained behind, tearless and stricken, to minister to the frankly helpless Edith. A brace of young aunts and a female cousin by marriage sighed and sniffed in the background. And still the newly made widow dominated the scene by her absence. And still Uncle Tom did not come.

2

He came, however, at four o'clock, when the others returned. He volunteered no explanation of his conduct, and no one had the courage to demand it of him. He looked to be, and was, a hale, elderly, and astute London solicitor. He dominated his brothers and sisters by the sheer force of his insensitiveness, his difference from themselves. Instinctively they turned to him, as to something solid, rather stupid, but thoroughly reliable. He offered, with his loud-voiced, matter-of-fact air, and his preoccupation with business matters, an asylum from sentiment. Among this older generation of Simpsons he alone had never dallied, however idly, with thoughts of art. Edward, compromising between ambition and necessity, had made himself a first-class poster-designer. Harry had secretly circulated among his friends a volume of pastoral poems. Frederick, having lost his way and strayed into the employ of a commercial firm, had hankered all his life to practise architecture. Even Elizabeth had a pretty talent for water-colour painting. But Tom, proud though he was of his mother's other children, was supremely content to be unlike them. He knew himself to be a highly successful professional man, and he was grimly happy in the knowledge. While others trifled with playthings of the mind, exploiting their own unimportant emotions, he shouldered the work of the world.

It was to execute a duty that he was here now, and for no idle purpose. Sincerely as he regretted his brother's death, there was a touch of exasperation in his regret. It was so like poor Fred, always a bit of a bungler, to get ill and die at the ridiculously early age of sixty-one. Tom's bearing, as they all took their seats at the tea-table, suggested not so much that a man's life had ended as that a business had gone irreparably wrong and that he, Tom, presiding over a creditors' meeting, was determined to make the best of a bad job.

'Yes,' he admitted to his sister Elizabeth, 'it was a great shock to me. Incompetent doctor, no doubt. How's Adela taking it?'

Elizabeth shook her head. 'Ah, I'm afraid she's very sadly, poor girl. And obstinate too,' added the old lady, with a nervous glance in the direction of Edith. 'Yes, my dear, a wee bit stubborn. She shuts herself in her room and just gives way.'

'H'm,' said Tom. His disapproval needed no emphasis.

'After all,' ventured Rose, timidly, 'we've got to go on, haven't we?'

'You're right, my love,' said Tom, with a glance of keen affection.

At this moment the door opened, and Mrs Simpson stood, a tall black figure of desolation, framed in the doorway. She paused before moving into the room. All eyes turned towards her, yet turned reluctantly, afraid to face her. All, except Edith who was too devoted, Elizabeth who was too wise, and Tom who was too complacent, felt themselves detected in a kind of disloyalty. They were conscious of having thought unkindly of her. She had shut herself away, with sorrow and mortification as her sole companions ; yet they, in their secret hearts, had suspected her, at the worst of hypocrisy, at the best of self-deceiving sentimentality. Those cold eyes that had flashed so often with scorn for her husband were now bloodshot with intemperate grief for him. Those thin lips that had so often implied that his existence was a burden to her, now quivered in resentment of his having been taken from her. Yet in vain did Rose try to harden her heart against this mother; and Edward, though he could not like his sister-in-law, was not so simple as to think he understood her. Even in the moment of criticizing her tragedy-airs, her too obvious exploitation of a sentiment to which her new status entitled her, he rebuked himself with the trite reminder that human emotions will not submit to tabulation. Hypocrisy there might be; but might there not be genuine grief as well? And who could say which was the more fundamental? Harry did not bother with such problems; the miscellany of junior aunts, uncles, and cousins savoured the drama of Adela's entry without analysing it; and Tom was unaware that any problem existed. He had summed up his brother's wife years before, and had placed her definitely in a category in his mind from which she would never escape. 'The woman's acting!' he said to himself; and was content to leave it at that.

If Adela Simpson was acting, Edith lost no time in responding to her cue. She pushed her untouched plate away, and ran to her mother's side, grasped her hand with tender solicitude, and murmured inaudibly. A storm of weeping seemed imminent, but Tom was in no mood to tolerate such a discomfort.

He came forward with hand outstretched.

'Well, Adela, how are you? Come along and have some of your own tea. I wanted to wait for you, but Edith insisted that we shouldn't. Regular martinet, your daughter, eh?'

He took masterful possession of Mrs Simpson, and led her to the table.

'And after tea,' added Uncle Tom, 'a few of us will get together and talk business.'

Mrs Simpson made one futile attempt to resist this domination. 'My fatherless girls . . .' she began.

'Are adequately provided for,' said Uncle Tom. 'The brown bread-and-butter, if you please, Rose! . . . Thank you, my dear.'

3

And after tea, obedient to a hint, all the juniors and cousins and relations-in-law left the house, leaving the leaders of the clan to talk business. Rose, at her own request, was absent from the conference; but she could not escape its consequences. She greeted her mother, an hour later, when that afflicted lady suffered herself to be led by Edith from the presence of the informative Tom. But Rose's greeting went unanswered, perhaps unnoticed. In her mother's eyes she read a familiar story. The anger that Simpson's death had magically transmuted into self-pity now flamed again in his widow's mien.

'Mother!' Rose cried. 'What is the matter?' She turned in her distress and bewilderment to Edith. 'What is it, Edith? What has happened?'

Edith, with a dumb gesture of helplessness, passed on. Rose repeated her question to Aunt Elizabeth.

'My dear,' said Aunt Elizabeth, 'it's time I went back home. Walk a little way to the station with me.'

'But what has made mother look so dreadful?'

'Nothing to worry about. . . . Wait while I get my things on.'

On the way to the station Rose learned the little that the old lady could tell her.

'Your mother said such hard, cruel things, my dear. I'm not sure I can forgive her. But I ought not to have gone without saying good-bye. No, that was wrong of me. It was indeed.'

Simpson had left a hundred pounds out of his meagre estate to an unknown woman : that was the salient fact that emerged from Aunt Elizabeth's confused account. 'And your mother, my dear, puts the very worst construction on it. Your Uncle Tom did his best to hide it. But she would know everything. And now she knows she doesn't like it.'

'But,' cried Rose, 'is Mother left unprovided for ? '

'Your mother has a pension from the firm, of course. And there's plenty besides. It's not the money. It's . . . it's . . . oh, you're not such a child as not to understand.'

'Yes, I understand,' confessed Rose. She understood : perhaps better than anyone she understood. But, somehow, she was unable to feel humiliated, indignant, at the possibility of her father's secret life. She was excited by the romantic suggestions of this dramatic disclosure ; she at once pitied her father, and envied him. And, above all, she was glad, defiantly glad, that there had been at least one flash of passionate poetry in his dull and thwarted existence. She could not imagine him as anything but the old man he had been for some ten years or more. Earlier memories were blurred. She saw him now as she had last seen him : a thin, emaciated old man, with a white stubbly beard beginning to grow in flesh that seemed frail as tissue-paper. She saw his hands beating a tremulous tattoo on the sheets of his bed ; she heard his gallant attempt at gaiety in response to her greeting. Such a kindly, helpless old man ; and so utterly at the mercy of the pain that racked him.

The broken voice of Aunt Elizabeth broke in upon her musing. 'Don't think ill of your dear father,' said Aunt Elizabeth. The next moment, 'Oh, Rose,' she cried, with trembling lip, ' he was such a pretty baby ! '

THE BENDING SICKLE

THE BENDING SICKLE

YOUNG Corbett returned from lunch just in time to open the door of his bank for a crooked old lady who appeared too feeble, or too timid, to effect an entry without aid. Her white wisps of hair straying from under a queer little bonnet, and the parchment pallor of her wrinkled skin, contrasted so oddly with the innocent blue of the eyes she turned towards him that for a brief moment the boy's heart faltered in the presence of unnameable premonition. There was a touch of gallantry, as well as of proprietorship, in the gesture with which, having ushered her in, he bestowed on her the freedom of the institution from which he received twenty-five shillings a week.

The old lady, leaning on her ebony stick, approached the bank counter with an air of profound resolution, and in a low voice made known her wishes to the cashier. Could she see the manager?

'I will see if he is disengaged,' said the cashier. 'What name may I say?'

'Eh?' She had failed to hear. 'I want him to take care of something for me.'

'Certainly. May I send in your name?'

She shook her head, and smiled wistfully. 'No, I haven't got it with me. It's in the taxi outside. Perhaps some one would be kind enough to carry it in for me. It's rather heavy, don't you see.'

The cashier seemed embarrassed.

'Perhaps that nice young man who opened the door for me . . . if he would be so good. A black tin box, but rather heavy, you know.'

Young Corbett was summoned, and despatched on this errand; and the cashier addressed himself once again to the task of discovering his client's name. Having at last succeeded, he did his best to look as though he had known it all the time.

'Of course! How forgetful of me!' he exclaimed, although he had in fact never seen this lady before. 'I'm afraid the manager is out at the moment, Mrs Severn. Perhaps you would like a word with our Mr Turner?'

Our Mr Turner had to be approached with some caution. He was a bald, kindly, obstinate old man, permanently embittered by the knowledge that he was an anachronism, a professional failure, fifteen years older than the manager under whom he worked.

'A Mrs Severn wants to see you, sir.'

Mr Turner turned a cold eye on the spoiler of his peace, and slightly shifted his position on the tall stool, across the back of which his long black coat-tails hung in rigid propriety. 'Where's the manager?'

'Out, sir.'

With extreme reluctance Mr Turner laid down his pen, adjusted his pince-nez, and rose.

In the manager's room he found Mrs Severn already seated. He became at once the embodiment of polite urbanity. The bank would be delighted to be of service to Mrs Severn. The deed-box should be deposited in the safe, and a receipt issued. Had Mrs Severn an account here? No? Ah yes, the late Mr Severn had had an account. Of course. He remembered it perfectly.

He pressed a bell-push on the manager's desk. Corbett answered the ring.

'Make out a safe-custody receipt for this box, contents unknown. The name is Mrs Severn. Let me see, have we your full name, Mrs Severn?'

'Cathleen,' said the old lady, when at last the question reached her. 'Cathleen Severn.'

'Thank you,' said Corbett, bowing, and went back into the outer office.

While they waited, the bank official and the client, for the return of Corbett with the receipt ready for signature, Mr Turner sat in pensive silence. Conversation with this lady was too difficult a matter ; and, indeed, he himself was rather hard of hearing. He allowed his thoughts to wander. Cathleen. How incongruously the name had sounded on the old lady's lips. Well, not so old perhaps, but oldish, oldish—like himself. Mr Turner was vaguely aware that Cathleen was a name which had once held some special significance for him. He could distinctly remember how, in his youth, he had never seen or heard it without an echo of an old emotion. He recalled the echo ; he recalled vaguely the emotion ; but whatever had first occasioned that emotion now eluded him.

2

Michael Antony Turner was twenty-one, a bank-clerk on holiday. Already he had spent three days of his fortnight's leave, and

spent them very profitably, as he considered :
solitary, cooking and cleaning for himself,
in a two-roomed cottage in Little Essex
situated on the left of the High Street where
it bends round the lower pool past the old
market-place, now disused. Much of his
time, and all his thought, had been given
not to these domestic affairs but to self-
perfection in the process of making wood-
cuts. He had brought with him, besides
the homespun suit he stood up in, three
extra shirts, five pairs of socks, two tooth-
brushes, a comb, and shaving tackle. All
these he had stowed into a haversack, too
new to be picturesque, of which he had been
intermittently conscious all the while it had
lain in the rack of the railway carriage. He
would have walked the long distance cheerfully ; indeed he would have delighted to
walk, exulting in sore heels and the adventure of sleeping in the lee of haystacks
and waking with farmyard smells in his nostrils. He was very much in earnest, very
innocent of affectation : a creature still dewy
with youth.

He stood in the post office, absently fingering a little oblong of thin paper which the girl
at the counter had given him in exchange for
a parcel. A self-conscious impulse made him

look up. In the girl's eyes the ghost of a surprised kindliness still lingered ; maternal amusement hovered about her mouth and slightly dimpled her cheek.

Michael's glance rested upon her with satisfaction. And while he stared, something unprecedented happened to him. She was tall, built on a generous scale, yet gracefully and perfectly proportioned. He noticed, with a curious spasm of surprise, her broad brow, the full and kindly contours of her face, the unique charm of blue eyes and dark hair. Where had he seen her before? He had never seen her before. Yet he felt this meeting to be at once an adventure and a homecoming ; he felt as an exile may feel when at a turn of the lonely road he comes upon some vision of meadow and sky that is intimate and dear, yet strange.

He blushed to find himself staring. ' Oh, and may I have a dozen stamps ? '

She smiled. Summer lightning played over her features, a tiny lyric of laughter too frail for sound. ' You may, surely. Is it any particular kind you're wanting ? '

When he had received his stamps and paid for them, they exchanged good morning, and he went out into the spring sunlight. The street was transfigured. Even the red letter-box, let into the post-office wall, had become an apocalypse of beauty. Back went Michael to his cottage, a three miles walk along country roads. His body moved on in a world that had the perfection of a work of art, but his mind remained exquisitely poised, contemplating the burning beauty whose limbs this visible creation did but transparently veil. 'Life of life . . .' He recited two stanzas of Shelley to the heedless hedges.

As he turned into the High Street of his village, he dodged across the road to avoid his loquacious landlord, old George Proudfoot. George was the most sensational feature of Little Essex. He resembled nothing so much as a blasphemous parody of God the Father. He was white-haired, saintly in appearance, and nearly always drunk. His obscene jests were the pride of three local taverns. But to-day Michael was in no mood for George.

He entered the cottage, lunched off bread and cheese, and dreamed his day away. Seven o'clock, closing time, found him back in the little provincial town again, hovering near the post office in hope of seeing her. But when at last she emerged she was accompanied by a friend, a dumpy girl, a parody of humankind. Michael, shamefaced but desperate, followed the two at a respectful distance through several streets, until a little grey villa engulfed them both.

The days of his leave sped on into the void, never to be recovered. That is how he himself thought of it. And then, with all the unexpectedness of crisis, he saw her again. With her dumpy friend she was entering a field where local sports were to be held. The place was gay with bunting, which floated, like the pennons of ships, over a sea of chatter and perspiration.

The two girls took up their stand on the outskirts of the crowd. There was a clear path to her. A sack-race was beginning. Michael had lived for twenty-one years without ever discovering before the consuming interest that a sack-race held for him. He expiated this neglect in an instant's enthusiasm.

He was at her side, raising his hat, blushing and murmuring. She acknowledged his existence coldly. The attendant goblin scowled. Then, with mutterings and furtive gestures, it began to scold. Michael's heart threatened to leap out of his body. Would these insulted young women call a policeman? But the mutterings and furtive gestures produced no visible effect in the face of deity.

Said Michael, reciting his rehearsed part:
'I wrote a letter to you yesterday.'
'Did you then?' Deity appeared amused. 'I haven't seen it.'
'No. I didn't post it. I couldn't, not knowing your name. I was on the way to the post office to deliver it by hand, when I saw you going into the enclosure here.'

She hesitated before asking: 'And the letter—what was it all about?'
'It was an apology.'
'Indeed?'
'Yes. It's very kind of you to pretend not to understand. It was disgraceful of me to follow you about the other night, quite unpardonable. But I couldn't help it.'
'Oh, that!' she said. 'I was awfully sorry about that. I'd no idea you meant to wait for me. It took me by surprise.'

He swam in a sea of delicious implications.

3

From that to the ultimate avowal was an inevitable step. They had walks and talks together, and at last, one day, after a morning's work, she was able to give him nine consecutive hours of her intoxicating company.

The day was radiant. They walked in a world of flame. To Michael it was as if she moved, a queen of beauty, amid the loveliness that she herself had created. He was extravagant, and he recognised his extravagance. He had never felt so idiotic and so happy. He felt himself to be alone with Cathleen in a beautiful, unreal universe. Only themselves, and his love for her, were real.

Their road led to a bridge that ran over a railway cutting. They climbed a gate and sat down, side by side, on the green dry turf of the embankment. The road arched over them. All things conspired to urge that this, and no other, was the supreme moment, the pivot upon which the whole world turned.

'I've got something to say,' he faltered.

'Yes.'

'And I'm dreadfully afraid, because, you see, I don't believe the things you believe, and . . .'

'You mean you're a Protestant,' she helped him out.

'No. I simply don't believe, that's all. I can't. And the terrible thing is . . .' He lost command of his voice. His heart beat dangerously. His face flamed.

She suddenly had hold of his hand and was caressing it with her own. 'Yes, I know,' she said soothingly, as to a little child.

'You see,' he went on, on the verge of tears, 'I'm so dreadfully in love with you.'

He had said it, and now she must answer him. The pause was an agony, but a beautiful agony.

'If only you were my religion,' she said.

He looked up. 'What did you say?'

'I wish you were a Catholic, like me, Michael.'

'You mean . . . ?'

'I couldn't marry any but a Catholic.'

He stared into his lap again and sighed. 'I thought so.'

'It isn't that I'm not very fond of you,' she said.

What angel from heaven could have said more? He turned, put his arm about her, and drew her towards him. Just as he was going to kiss her she turned away her head.

Their eyes met. 'Mustn't I?'

She shook her head, but her eyes were tender. 'No. I'd never kiss a boy I'd not be marrying.'

'It doesn't matter,' he said. Without argument he waived his claim.

'It isn't that I'm not fond of you,' she

repeated, fearing he was hurt. 'It's a promise I made, a vow. I couldn't break it.'

Michael stroked her hand. 'It's all right. I'm not worrying because I mustn't kiss you. I'll do anything you say. It's this other trouble. I want to marry you. Oh God, I want to marry you, Cathleen!'

'And I want you to, Michael. Won't you try to be a Catholic? If I give you a prayer, will you say it? God will change your unbelief, and everything will be all right.'

'You don't understand, my dear. I can't pray. It would be hypocrisy. I don't believe there's anyone to pray to.'

'What a wicked boy you are!' cried Cathleen, fondly scolding.

'But, Cathleen, listen. You don't understand how I feel about these things. I must be faithful to my convictions, mustn't I?'

'Not if they're wrong,' she said firmly. The shadow of despair darkened his face. 'Never mind, dear Michael. Let's be happy while we can.'

'Let's go and get some tea.' He rose, and helped her up.

There was a moment of sweet anguish for Michael when, in the teashop, the landlady had left them to themselves, and he watched

Cathleen pour out the tea. He had never before sat with her in such domestic intimacy; nor seen her with her hat off. He imagined themselves married and in their own home, and the longing to kiss her lips almost overwhelmed him. Almost, but not quite. Cathleen allowed him to enfold her, to touch her cheek with his own. With his smooth face he stroked the down, the marvellous bloom, of her white neck. Tantalising himself, he put his lips to hers in the shadow of a kiss. And yet he did not kiss her.

4

Subsequent days brought more hours of poignant joy. Michael's leave dwindled to vanishing point. When he and Cathleen were together, not even the thought of approaching doom, the death-in-life of separation, could quench their delight in each other. Like waifs tossed together in mid-ocean, they clung in bliss until the unappeasable tides of the world should come to cleave them for ever asunder. So Michael saw their situation; but Cathleen was buoyed up by a secret belief which he, more clear-sighted, could not entertain. She believed that sooner or later her Michael would find his way into the arms of the one true Church, and so into her own arms never to be loosed.

The last day of the world dawned in splendour. She was shut up in her post office, he knew, until seven o'clock; but at five, unable to endure another moment's inactivity, he stepped out of his cottage and turned his face towards her.

Ten yards away, he met her. His heart shouted with joy. She had got time off for him. They had two hours added to their precious evening. . . . But a second glance at her face checked his ecstasies.

'Oh, Michael!'

'Darling, what is it?'

'I've got to do telegraphs to-night.'

Before she could continue he cried out, 'Telegraphs! Is our last night to be laid waste by telegraphs!' Despair, like a cold toad, sat upon his heart.

'Sally has been called away.' Sally was the dumpy friend. 'Her mother's very ill.'

'The goblin! Do goblins have mothers?'

'Don't be cruel, Michael. I must be back at closing time.'

'Come back to the cottage,' he said, preoccupied with disappointment. 'Unless you'd rather walk?'

She looked at him gravely, trying to veil the surprise in her eyes ; and she knew at once that he did not realise the magnitude of what he had asked of her. Such innocence could only be matched by generosity, no matter what it cost her.

'No,' she answered firmly. 'I'd rather sit down.' But she could not repress a pang of fear as she entered the cottage door. Had she been seen ? Was her reputation already being butchered by the village gossips ?

Once inside, alone with her joy and her pain, she cast fear aside. Time slipped away, and it seemed to Michael that all the best of life, all beauty, all delight, was slipping with it. Cathleen sat on a hassock at his feet and rested her head in his lap. With the bitterness of parting already in his mouth, he felt upon his shoulders all the illimitable tragedy of life—exquisite burden. Here was his one chance of love, and it was passing. To-morrow he would be too old for love.

He bent over her yearningly, raised her a little in his arms ; and his hands fondled her firm full breasts. He felt himself drowning in the bliss of her body's loveliness.

'O Cathleen, do love me !'

She looked up, tender, distressed, struggling with herself. 'I'm crazy about you, Mick. Kiss me!' For an immortal moment she yielded her lips to him with passion.

He became divinely mad. 'Love me! Do love me!'

She had given all she dared. 'I must really go now. Let me go, darling!'

She rose; tidied her hair; put on her hat. They kissed again, in farewell.

'You'll write to me, Michael?'

'Yes, I'll write,' he said, still trembling.

They tried to smile at each other.

'O Michael, I must tell you. I thought to hide it, but I can't. I'm being transferred to Ireland next month. The order came through yesterday.'

To Michael, pent in the city of London, Ireland would be infinitely remote. He could not speak.

'But we must meet again, mustn't we? You'll say that prayer I gave you, Michael? Then everything will come right for us.'

He wanted to cry out 'Go! Go!' But he still smiled with grey lips. 'I'll try, Cath.'

'Good-bye.'

'Good-bye.'

She was gone, out of sight at last. Michael

stepped back to his cottage door, staggered against the lintel, and hid his face from the light. He felt utterly beaten and forlorn, like an abandoned child. Yet when, the first fury of grief spent, he went into his bedroom, it was not the face of a child that he saw in the mirror but that of a haggard youth, with age in his eyes and dark semicircles under them.

He went to the window and leaned out towards the horizon. Hours passed without sound. The sky hung over him like a luminous curtain of green shading into a less luminous blue, in which one tiny puncture, the first star, flashed and faded and flashed again like a dagger's point. The infinite spaces were emptied of meaning for him; mute and still, they were but the symbol of an everlasting indifference. The evening light seemed unearthly, tinting all things with a colour that made the green grass darkly vivid and the hedges a dim purple. In the field just below him, beyond the patch of kitchen-garden, old George Proudfoot bent over his mowing, pausing from time to time to spit on his hands and stare at the world's rim. For a moment Michael's glance rested on that ancient man, dignified only in labour ; and in the boy's unlistening ears sounded the sibilant unfaltering rhythm of moving sickle and falling grass.

5

In the Manager's Room of the City and Counties Bank, Oxford Street, old Mr Turner, with a polite official expression fixed on his well-preserved, clean-shaven face, spent ten seconds or less in his endeavour to recall the peculiar significance of his client's Christian name. Other thoughts soon wandered aimlessly across his mind. His wife that morning had had the beginnings of a cold in the head. He hoped it had not developed. Annie was tiresome when anything ailed her : apt to sigh with unnecessary emphasis, and to make allusions, none too veiled, to his ill-success in business. She had wanted the eldest boy sent to Oxford ; she had wanted all manner of unattainable things. And she sniffed. It was always a discomfort having people with colds about the house. A pity she sniffed. A pity she bullied her servant. Yet she was necessary : the thought of life without her was not to be entertained. They had ways and tastes and a handful of ideas in common. Each to the other was an ineradicable habit, and he recognised the fact not only without bitterness but with a certain positive satisfaction.

Corbett interrupted his musing by bringing in the safe-custody receipt made out for his signature. Corbett, smart junior, had been out of the room a bare three minutes, during which time neither Mr Turner nor his venerable client had said a word. Mr Turner, once more the complete bank official, affixed his signature with an accustomed gesture.

'And that is your receipt, Mrs Severn.'

'Thank you,' she said, receiving it from his hand. Laboriously she read it through. She rose to her feet unsteadily, helped by her stick. 'I do hope my taxi hasn't run off without me.'

Mr Turner opened the door for her. 'Allow me,' he said, presenting his arm.

They passed out together into the public office. When they reached the swing-doors that gave upon the street he stood aside to let her pass out; then followed to escort her to the waiting taxi.

Seated in the taxi, she bent forward to thank him. He bowed courteously over her mittened hand, and looking up met the glance in her blue eyes. 'So kind of you,' she said. 'I'm not so young as I was, Michael.'

The taxi had moved away before it occurred

to him to wonder. For a few moments he stood, lost in dreams ; then he went back to his duties. 'Well, well, well,' said Mr Turner. 'Now *there's* a strange thing.'

ATTITUDES

ATTITUDES

THE morning's post, brought to his bedside by an indulgent mother, did not yield the treasure for which he had hungered these ten days past, but it contained the next best thing, a letter from Tommy Barnard, who was in the know about other things than stocks and shares.

'Would you like your breakfast in bed, dear?'

A young man who teaches modern languages at a public school is entitled to such maternal attentions, especially during the last week of his vacation. Brian Hunter was not astonished. He was polite, though preoccupied.

'No, thanks, mother. I'll be down in a jiffy.'

In cold fact he detested taking breakfast in bed. Until washed and shaved he felt neither equal to the effort nor worthy of the reward. He was reluctant even to open a letter until he was cleansed of sleep, but Tommy's impulsive caligraphy promised excitement that he could not resist. He broke the seal ; he delicately extracted a sheet of pale-blue notepaper ; and the astounding news leapt up at him. 'Caroline's engagement,' wrote Tommy Barnard, in his dry, malicious fashion, ' comes as a surprise to me—though not, I expect, to you, who were in her confidence. Shall we lunch together to-morrow . . .' With studied deliberation Hunter replaced the letter in its envelope and strode into the bathroom. Above all, he must not lose his head, or his dignity. He must be normal. There were three Carolines of his acquaintance, but he refused, manfully, to delude himself with doubting that this was his own Caroline, the one great passion of his life, she who had been his inspiration and his mistress for what seemed a lifetime, though it was in fact rather less than five months. A stricken man, he turned on the bath tap and stared, unseeing, at the pouring water. Visions besieged his mind ; he pressed sensitive fingers to his eyes ; his left hand clutched the edge of the bath. When he uncovered his face he could not avoid noticing that the bath was not plugged ; the cold water was running out as fast as it poured in. With mournful satisfaction he recognised his mistake and corrected it. This would never do. On no account must he lose his self-command.

His toilet completed without further mishap, his breakfast deedily consumed and his mother's curiosity circumvented, he hastened to the appointed place to meet Tommy Barnard. They lunched, frugally but not inexpensively, in a wine house near Fleet Street. The place was full of men murmuring together. Tommy pointed out a plump poet engaged in conversation with a wistful advertising man, mentioned their names and added, not without unction : 'They're often here. It's a good place. Only one fault, in fact. Too many women.' There was no woman visible, but Hunter was not surprised by the remark. Tommy Barnard was a dark horse, and often meant more than he said, especially when he said what was palpably untrue ; on such occasions one had to search, and search hard, for an inner meaning. But Hunter, in the grip of his desolation, had at the moment no thought to spare for such things. If he caught himself being interested in his surroundings he pulled himself up short. He stared at his friend expectantly. Above the murmurous confusion of sounds rose a clear, youthful voice precisely and solemnly articulating : 'No, seriously, Ernest ! Where *do* you get your ties ? I'm not joking, dear old friend. I really want to know.' A waiter appeared, and Barnard woke from a profound lethargy to give his order.

Hunter continued to watch him, and as the minutes passed in silence he became vaguely oppressed by the man's fatness and floridity and incipient baldness. He liked old Tommy, and had always been amused by the air of seasoned depravity he affected, and by that cynicism about women which contrasted so sharply with his own view. This last was a sign of youth in the dear old chap; Hunter himself, though fifteen years his junior, had passed through the cynical period that closes adolescence and now reposed in a state of clear-eyed toleration. But to-day he found himself wishing that Tommy Barnard were a shade less bibulous. With a manner so casual, and a personal appearance so positively gross, small wonder that the poor fellow found himself unpopular with women and therefore, in sheer self-defence, affected to disdain them.

'Well,' said Hunter. 'I got your letter.'

Barnard smiled wanly. 'So I inferred from your presence here.' His fat hands made a gesture.

'What's all this about Caroline?'

'She's engaged to be married, old man.'

'Yes?' Hunter could not help feeling a twinge of pride in himself for the restraint of that monosyllable. 'And to whom?'

'To a man called Courcy. Know him?'

'Courcy?'

'Simple faith *and* Norman blood,' said Barnard. 'A combination Tennyson never dreamed of.'

'When did you learn this?'

'Yesterday. My wife told me. But it's all over the town. You hadn't heard?'

'No.'

'I'm sorry, Brian,' said Barnard. 'I'm damned sorry.'

'Yes, I know.' Hunter was embarrassed by this expression of sympathy. 'It's not the . . . the cutting adrift I mind so much. That was all, so to speak, in the contract. It was always understood that we were free, both of us. But there's a way of doing these things. There's a decent way, and there's a vulgar, mannerless way.'

Barnard nodded. 'I agree, my dear chap. She's treated you badly.'

'Courcy?' said Hunter. 'Isn't he that red-haired fellow with a squint and two thousand a year?'

'The very same.'

'Then I venture to say that Caroline is a person of very facile emotions. Why, only the last time I saw her, a fortnight ago, she declared that nothing would ever induce her to marry.'

'She overlooked the compelling power of a squint,' remarked Barnard. 'Have another drink?'

'Yes,' said Hunter. He eyed his glass sombrely. 'Lots of it. . . . She was quite amusing about it, I remember. She said that she made it a rule never to get married, but that if ever she admitted an exception it should be in my favour. What fun, eh?'

Barnard smiled, but without conviction. 'I'm glad you haven't lost your sense of humour, Brian.' And Brian himself couldn't help feeling that he deserved the compliment. 'I always thought you took that girl much too seriously. She was not, to be frank, quite all you imagined her.'

'Indeed?"

'I mean it. Do you remember that night at the Mandersons' dance, when you sat out five dances with her in the conservatory?'

'Do I remember?' said Hunter, grimly ironical. That night shone like a jewel among his memories: it was the night of all nights, the dawn of a great passion, the beginning of a new life, the re-birth of the soul. 'I rather fancy I do remember, Tommy.'

'Very well,' said Barnard. 'Then listen. Less than a fortnight before, about ten days, in fact, I happened to call at Caroline's flat.'

Hunter nodded receipt of this information, and waited to hear more. Since no more appeared to be forthcoming, he asked : ' What did you do that for ? '

' My dear Brian,' said Barnard, bracing himself for a further effort, ' I do hope you won't let this interfere with our friendship.'

' What did you go to her flat for ? ' persisted Brian, ignoring this irrelevance. ' Anyhow, why shouldn't you ? '

' Her dear sister was away,' said Barnard. ' She fancied herself in love. I lost my head. And—well, let's leave it at that, old man.'

Hunter felt his universe crumbling about him. The smiling face of his past assumed the leer of insanity. But still something within him reiterated that he must not lose command of himself. He must not ; but indeed he could not. If only he could have done so ! If only he had been able to relieve his pent feelings in violence ! But he was hemmed in on every side, as his mind was quick to perceive : too fastidious to indulge in melodramatic gestures, too fairminded to blame this middle-aged lout for what, after all, could not be accounted treachery. He suffered the more because of his sophistication. That, in spite of this gigantic upheaval, he remained a rational man, impeccably just, was a nuisance ; but it pro-

vided a fascinating spectacle. Yet when his
thought passed from himself to Caroline the
knife at his heart thrust more shrewdly ; thrust
and twisted and drew the blood from his
cheeks. Looking up he encountered the
solicitous gaze of Barnard, and the red tide
rushed back.

For the sake of saying something he murmured lamely : 'Don't mind me. It's a bit
of a shock.'

'You realise,' said Barnard, ' that since then,
since you came on the scene, there has been
nothing of that sort . . . nothing at all.'

'That goes without saying,' answered
Hunter. 'I blame you for nothing, except,
perhaps, for not having warned me.'

Barnard shrugged his shoulders. 'I had
no right to do that. I had no right to tell you
to-day. But I believed it would do you good
to know the truth. You think you're very
much a man of the world, Brian, but you're
really a child. There was no sense in letting
you nurse a romantic sorrow all your life.'

'Very well. Let's have a drink, shall we ?
I'm feeling rather like Leontes at the moment,
but it will pass.' To be crushed by misfortune,
humiliated, stung to savage jealousy—it was a
disgusting but interesting experience. 'I'm
not going to let this thing smash me up,' he

added, with a wry smile. 'I've just got to readjust myself to this new idea, that's all. At present everything's topsy-turvy. It's just as if somebody had died, and I can't quite believe it. In fact, somebody has died, the Caroline I knew.'

'She never existed,' Barnard put in.

'No, you're right. And that's the desolating thing. All that she said and did was just . . . make-believe.'

They discussed the matter upside down and inside out. They continued to drink until they were the only people left in the place. The journalists had gone their ways; the juvenile epicure in neckties had returned to his own place. Hunter clung with all his weight to the blessed word, readjustment; it comforted him; it obscurely flattered him. Caroline, to all intents and purposes, was dead. But Caroline, as he had conceived her, had never lived. How could one mourn the death of a romantic fancy? Yet mourn he did. Bitterness overwhelmed him.

Barnard rose.

'Going?' said Brian. 'Not yet, surely?'

'Stocks must be broked though kingdoms fall,' answered Barnard, employing a facetious formula of his. 'Of course, you academic chaps . . ,'

Barnard drifted back to his office, leaving poor Troilus without an audience. Memories invaded that solitude, memories that inflamed and derided him ; but after a while the roses and raptures began to be blotted out by the irritating recollection of a day which, now that he paused to examine his past, seemed only too characteristic of the progress of that mighty passion. In imagination he lived again every minute of that day.

It was a day spent largely in call-offices, telephoning here and there in quest of Caroline, with intervals of anguished waiting at a certain club, waiting for a call from her. It was there at last that he heard her eager voice, soft, clear, delicately self-possessed. ' I shall be in at two. Yes, at my flat. Hetty is out for the afternoon.' Hetty was the stupid elder sister in whom it was impossible to confide. Hetty represented that antiquated morality which he and Caroline so gladly and gracefully disavowed. Both sisters had artistic gifts, which they were busily cultivating ; but Caroline's fiddling was more rapacious in its demands than Hetty's painting. So at half-past one he walked boldly into the flat, having opened the door with his own latchkey. The first sight that greeted his eyes was Hetty on her way downstairs. ' Hullo, Mr Hunter ! How did you manage to get in ?' Hunter explained that he had found the front door ajar, enquired politely after Caroline, and was invited to sit down and await her return. After ten minutes of purgatorial small talk, Hetty began apologising for the dullness of her conversation. 'The fact is,' she said, 'I'm a little put out. I was to have met an old friend this afternoon. We were going to have a jolly day in the Manuscript Room at the British Museum. But just before you arrived I had a wire putting it all off.' In due time Caroline appeared, dark, slim, exquisite. Poor Brian waited with held breath to see how she would handle the situation. 'Why not treat yourself to a matinee, Hetty?' she suggested, with sisterly solicitude. 'I'll treat us all to a matinee,' cried Hetty brightly. 'Oh *do* come, Mr Hunter ! We shall be *so* offended if you don't.'

Such were Hunter's memories of illicit love.

The affair had enormously disturbed and complicated his life ; during all these months he had thought about little else. The young lovers had been very earnest and self-analytical. Much as they deplored the need for concealment and deceit, which indeed was a constant exasperation, they faced it courageously, knowing the alternatives to be separation, which was unthinkable, and marriage, which was scarcely less so. Caroline was emphatic, almost devout, in her repudiation of the idea of marriage, which she regarded as both gauche and dishonourable : a form of surrender to the smug world, a settling down, the beginning of the end. She was ambitious to become a great violinist, and in Hunter's opinion was within an ace of achieving the ambition. In the circumstances he agreed, though with less enthusiasm, that marriage was out of the question . . . ' for the moment,' he added in his secret heart.

And now, with no Barnard to restrain him, he gave rein to his thoughts. He climbed up into the street, which blazed with sunlight, and boarded a homeward bus, upon which he rode, consciously tragic, like an aristocrat of France on his way to the guillotine. He sat with bared head and gazed proudly at the passing street below ; and his response was mechanical when the conductor of the tumbril came to demand a sixpenny fare. The motor-engine throbbed out a requiem for his dead love. Phrases of the letter he would write to Caroline began speaking in his mind. It should be very gentle, that letter, and very cold : ' I realise now that you did not mean a word of it—not a word, not a touch. But your acting was magnificent, and for that I am grateful.' Would that do ? No, it did

not strike quite the right note. The opening
was the least bit sentimental ; the irony of the
close might perhaps be missed. And it was
important, for her own soul's sake, that she
should know herself to be unmasked at last.
He tried again ; he warmed to the task. ' I
realise now that during all these wonderful
months you have been only striking attitudes.
But they were very elegant attitudes, and I
congratulate you on the performance.' That
was better. That struck at her unforgivable
sin, that habitual insincerity by which he had
allowed himself to be deceived. He recalled
the lyrical, stammering sentences with which
they had worshipped each other ; he felt her
little clinging hands upon his shoulders, and
lost himself in the infinite innocence and candour of her brown eyes. It was hard to
believe that she had meant nothing of what
those eyes had seemed to say, nothing of what
those lips had told his own. Could it be that
with all her posturing she was yet sincere ?
Could she have been herself deceived by her
own attitudes ? For an instant Hunter turned
the searchlight upon himself ; but there was
no profit in that enquiry and he did not pursue
it. Better to degrade her in his thoughts,
since she was now lost to him. It was all over
now, all the rapture, all the contriving, all the

elaborate subterfuge he had had to practise at home. The bus ride, too, was over ; and he strode down the road with buoyant step.

He was surprised, and a little shocked, to hear himself whistling. The gay notes, caught in their misdemeanour, trailed off guiltily into silence. His face clouded again ; his gaze grew wistful and dim as he contemplated his lost paradise. The terrible splendour of life and the beauty of his own emotions brought tears to his eyes, but he brushed them away with an impatient gesture and composed himself to meet his mother. He was free at last. He was desolated. The great experience of his life was over, and he was free to take an interest in other things. He must readjust himself to the new order, keeping the strong tides of his emotion under stern control.

He let himself into his mother's house, and, curiously lighthearted, ran to the drawing-room to take a cup of tea with her.

Mrs Hunter smiled up at him from her easy chair ; he kissed her playfully on the brow.

' Got any pretty cakes for me, mother ? '

' What a child it is ! ' she said contentedly. ' There's a letter for you, dear. It's on the mantelpiece.'

While she poured out a cup of tea for him,

he picked up his letter. His mouth set hard as he scrutinised the envelope; his knees trembled. And so she had written at last, after ten days' significant silence. She could tell him nothing that he did not already know, but he was glad that she had the good manners, the good taste, to make an end of things with some sort of dignity. She was reinstated in his respect. Careless of his mother's presence he tore open the letter and read: 'Dearest, dearest, dearest! It is all a hideous mistake. It seems to have got all over London that I am engaged to Leonard Courcy. It was true yesterday, but it's not true to-day. I want to see you *at once* and tell you everything. I have been dreadfully worried. You will get this by the three o'clock delivery, won't you? Come to me without delay. I shall be waiting, and alone. I shall pack Hetty off somewhere— I've told her all that she ought to know—and, would you believe it, she's positively sympathetic. Do come quickly.' Hunter stuffed the letter into his pocket and stood waiting, somewhat impatiently, for an ebullition of joy within him. For the great experience of his life was apparently not over, after all.

'Drink your tea before it's cold,' admonished Mrs Hunter.

'Right ho! Can't stay long.'

He could not bear to face the disappointment in his mother's look.

'Going out again?' she asked mildly.

'Yes. Awfully sorry. Got to see a man.'

He gulped his tea. He nibbled a fancy cake. He had to begin the task of readjustment all over again. It had been a fatiguing day.

MRS PUSEY'S CHICKENS

MRS PUSEY'S CHICKENS

ON a summer afternoon towards the close of the last century, when could still be found men of thirty who had never used a razor, a vehicle drawn by an elderly grey nag arrived to enliven the main street in a little Leicestershire village. It contained three souls. Confined in the same cab, moving down the same cobbled street, each of the three had yet a private world that impinged but superficially on that of either of the others.

Old Mrs Downes, despite her boasted energy, was already a little withdrawn from contact with her material environment, already inclined to slip away from the present into a placid browsing dream in which the events of her life moved to and fro in no chronological sequence. She was a child playing with her numerous sisters ; she was a young woman, wooed by a handsome young gentleman-farmer ; she was bringing forth her children ; she was riding with her husband over the cool white roads of evening. To her mind, when she allowed it so to dream, these things were equi-distant ; nor was their distance great : it was enough only to impart to them the colour of an added emotion, a not unpleasing sadness. It was as if, turning over the pages of her memory, she read again the long tale of herself, tenderly yet half-detached, as one might read in age any book associated intimately with one's remembered youth. It was indeed her own book and no other's, the book which she had daily, hourly, from moment to moment, all unconsciously written, and to which she was still adding. At one time the touch of the elements, the sights and sounds of life, had had power to intoxicate her, so that she tingled with the ardour of stretching out her lovely arms to embrace the beauty of the world ; the present moment had glowed for her with its own light, intrinsically precious ; she had looked neither before nor after. But now the fingers of experience that played upon her were apt to be forgotten in the profound and intricate music they evoked ; their immediate physical caress passed instantly out of consciousness, but the harmonics of memory went on vibrating, trembling, down all the octaves of her long past. Every new season—whether vital spring, the burning pageant of summer, autumn that is like a melancholy phrase, or winter with its menacing asperity—came to her laden with the hoarded riches and alarms of her former seasons. The sun warming her aged hands, and the moon that shone through the curtained window to make perforated patterns on her bedroom wall, were lost, not seldom, in contemplation of the suns and moons of other years. She was aware that this cab-ride held for them all some special meaning ; but, locked in herself, she had at the moment no thought to spare for it.

Bernard, being five years old, had thought for nothing else. To him this old lady was a monstrous phenomenon in whose presence he was always the least little bit uneasy. He did not speculate upon her mystery, having better things to do : as an intellectual problem it did not exist for him, but as a sensation he was aware of it. Inclined to be intimidated by her magnificent remoteness, her taciturnity, her great bulk and the pendulous parchment-flesh of her long face, he stared up at her from time to time with wide-eyed, impersonal curiosity. Even in her elastic-sided boots, and in the crimped and innumerably beaded black material with which she was identified rather than clothed, he found a vague inimical significance. That she was over eighty years old, as he had often heard said, meant nothing to him. Her difference from others was one not of age but of kind; and the immense respect with which she was treated served to enhance her awfulness. She was to be cajoled, persuaded, propitiated; disobeyed, perhaps, but never defied; circumvented but never contradicted; and to these ends there existed a conspiracy in which he himself—as it flattered him to remember—made common cause with his mother, with Miff-Miff, his grandmother's tame dragon or lady-companion, and with the two servants of the household. It was the affectionate but erratic Miff-Miff herself— only to tradesmen and to pedants was she known as Miss Smith—who had instructed him in the secret code of how to behave towards Granny. Unaware of the everlasting flux that would in time sweep even him, if he lived, into a similar state of mysterious and semi-impotent majesty, he saw his grandmother as a fixed fact of existence, solid and static like the tall brick wall that surrounded her garden and supported delicious apricot trees. She, like his mother and his father, had always been the same. He himself was growing up, as wellmeaning persons incessantly reminded him; but in this respect he was unique, the only active principle in a universe of unchanging things.

If Mrs Downes was a little unreceptive to the charms of the external world, Bernard was perhaps too small a vessel to contain them. Bewildered by the adventure of riding in a cab through a strange village, he could not eat fast enough of the feast life was spreading for him. There were so many equal claims on his attention that he could not possibly do full justice to them all : the thatched cottages flying past, the sunlight dancing in the cab, the springy motion, the rolling wheels, the complicated clop-clop on the cobblestones of four equine feet, and the pervading smell of plush and warm pegamoid. These things constituted the very delirium of delight, to which the presence of Granny contributed a spiritual flavour that was a little more than strange and a little less than astringent.

The third member of the party, and the link between these two extremes, was Mary Durham, daughter and mother. To Granny she was still, at times, the baby and darling of the family ; at other times she was a strange young woman who had unaccountably dispossessed her of that same baby-girl, and whom it was difficult to forgive for the depredation. To herself she was wife of one boy and mother of another, and beginning to be aware of her forty years. To Bernard she was half the world ; plump, placid, golden-haired ; the incarnation of comfort, the most important of all his possessions. Next in order of importance, if not of affection, came Dear Nana, his personal bodyguard at home ; and it is a nice problem (though it did not exercise Bernard himself) whether the third place should go to Father or to Ferdinand, the wooden donkey. Father was, perhaps, of more practical use ; but Ferdinand was better-tempered. Father had jokes and games and long whiskers to recommend him, to say nothing of a fat loud-ticking watch ; but, on the other hand, Father's jokes were not always of the first quality, his appetite for games was not insatiable, and sometimes he chose to persist in silly questions when a fellow wished to be quiet and think about life. At such times to ride a-cock horse to Banbury Cross was a misdirection of energy ; and even the pleasure of tugging at bushy brown whiskers proved to be a pleasure that could pall. Ferdinand, though less articulate, was more intelligent. He could frisk and gallop and canter, and leap over the bristling battlements of castles ; but he knew, with super-asinine intuition, just when the game should stop and a new one be begun. He responded to the slightest hint, trotted into his stable in the toy-cupboard without a word of protest : a trick Father had never learnt. Now Mother had, in effect, learnt it ; and to this, perhaps, among other and deeper things, she owed her enthronement in Bernard's heart.

Mary Durham's thoughts oscillated between her son and her absent husband. This visit to the home of her one surviving parent, where with Bernard she had already spent a week, was the first since her marriage seven years ago. Mrs Downes had chosen to oppose the match ; had made the tactical error of positively forbidding it ; and had never acknowledged the accomplished fact. But Mary, though she had a firmer grasp upon the present than either her mother or her son, recognised certain inevitabilities. The very phrase, 'eighty-four years old,' was to her like a sentence of death ; and to all on whom that shadow has visibly fallen one must be generous. So it was that she had written, with no reference to the seven years' silence broken only by annual letters, coolly announcing her intention of coming to stay. Up to now the holiday had been unmarred by audible discord, unglorified by full reconciliation. Bernard's father loomed always upon the horizon of their thoughts, tactfully keeping his distance yet undeniably existing : an amiable, ineffectual person, a tradesman and the son of a tradesman, and—in Mrs Downes's view—a stepping-stone to lower things.

For Bernard this holiday at Granny's had been a time of boundless, untroubled delight : long summer days in which he had wandered about the house and the incredible garden in busy silence. 'Are you happy, dear?' his mother would ask him, looking a little anxiously into his dream-laden eyes ; and responding to the invitation of her outstretched hands he would put his arms round her neck and cling to her for a moment, before running away with his head full of more pressing concerns. He did not answer her question, being too happy to understand it. Bernard had provided the two women with occasion for their one overt quarrel. Granny insisted that it was high time the child went to school, where his wilful fancy would be checked.

'One can't believe a word he says, my dear,' said the old lady. 'He's nearly six, and he seems sixty. When he stares at me with those absurd solemn eyes of his, why, I feel quite kittenish by contrast.'

'You don't mean he's . . . untruthful, mamma?'

'What else should I mean?' blandly enquired Mrs Downes.

'Oh, I'm sure he doesn't tell real stories,'

Bernard's mother was plaintive in his defence.
'He says strange things, but all children do.
It's imagination. It's a kind of . . .' Mary
Durham blushed at the word in her mind, and
feared to utter it lest thereby she should destroy
her secret hope. But the word refused to be
withheld. 'A kind of poetry.'

Granny wrinkled up her nose and lips into
an expression of extreme distaste. 'Poetry !
I don't want anything like that in *my* family.
I know your poets. Look at Byron—the
young scamp !'

'But there's Mrs Hemans, mamma, and . . .'

'I dare say there is. Send the boy to
school, my dear. What's that husband of
yours thinking of, I'd like to know.'

'Which husband of mine ?' Her mother's
daughter was beginning to stir in Mary.

Mrs Downes simulated alarm. 'Eh ?
What's that ? You've only one, I hope !'

'I expect you mean Ted,' said Mary primly.
'Well, Ted leaves it to me to look after Bernard. I'm his mother, after all.'

'Ah !' Mrs Downes's eyes shone with
pleasure in herself. 'They're all alike. They
get the child, and leave the rest to you.'

'There's no need to be vulgar, mamma.'

But Mrs Downes, having quarrelled herself
into a state of juvenile exhilaration, smiled

benignly on her daughter, who smiled back with equal candour and affection. They had a great respect for each other, these two ; but each underrated the other's capacity to forgive. And each was conscious that the healing word had yet to be spoken. That Bernard was the ostensible subject of this little disagreement deceived neither of them : Bernard's father had called it into being. Mary understood her mother's intention but not her motive. The older woman had not recanted her original seven-year-old heresy ; the younger had not embraced it. Beneath their surface friendliness was mutual resentment ; but beneath the resentment was something that drew them together. Pride made them enemies, but love cleansed their enmity of malice.

2

The cab came to a standstill ; and Bernard and his mother stepped into the brilliant day. Mrs Downes, fatigued by the ride, silently elected to stay and rest. As they stood, mother and son, waiting for Jinny to open her cottage door to them, the sunlight seemed to percolate through every pore of Mary's skin until her whole being brimmed with the golden wine. Yet a faint misgiving trembled on the threshold of her heart. This was the scene, and Jinny the friend, of her early childhood ; both for many years unvisited. Eager to renew those unforgotten vital sensations, she was yet reluctant to read what the fingers of time must have written on the familiar face. This fear flashed upon her for the first time as she heard the latch being lifted from the other side. The village, the cottage : these shewed no change. These things of stone remained, and would remain, long after the hearts that loved them had ceased to beat, and the eyes to shine. Ostensibly for Bernard's pleasure, secretly to indulge her private sentiment, this visit had been planned. At the last moment a shadowy premonition urged her to return to the cab, to cease troubling the still waters of memory, to relinquish this attempt to invade the inviolable past. But, before she could obey, the door opened.

A little and wizened old woman stood blinking at the visitors. The colour of her leathern face contrasted strikingly with her white wisps of hair, neatly parted in the middle and falling in the shape of an inverted V over her brow.

Mary, as if a cold hand had touched her, shivered involuntarily. Then she smiled with a certain tenderness. ' It *is* Mrs Pusey, isn't it ? '

'Eh?' The old woman rubbed a pair of gaunt hands on her apron. Mary repeated the question, raising her voice. 'That's me,' said Mrs Pusey.

'Why, don't you remember me, Jinny? Don't you remember Mary Downes?'

Mrs Pusey shook her head. 'I know what it is,' she said, with a kind of vindictiveness. 'Something's 'appened to my George. There's always something 'appening to poor folks.'

'No,' Mary assured her. 'I haven't come with bad news, Jinny. I just thought I'd come to see how you were getting on, you who were so kind to me when I was a little girl. Don't you remember?'

'Come inside, marm. No one can't say I haven't got a good memory. Wonderful for me age as they all tell me, which is seventy seven come Michaelmas. What did you say your name was, marm?'

'Mary Durham now,' said Bernard's mother, blushing slightly. 'But it was Mary Downes when you last saw me.'

'So you're Mary Downes, are you!' Mrs Pusey nodded with an air of singular shrewdness. 'Of course you are, my dear. I never forget a face. Not me.'

She renewed her invitation to enter, and this time remembered to validate it by opening the door wider. Bernard, at the sight that met him, was aghast with joy. The kitchen, red-tiled and impeccably clean, was aswarm with little fluffy yellow creatures, waddling balls of gold. Their aliveness made him cry out his delight; but after that one sound he remained silent, filling his eyes with the ecstasy.

Forgetting Jinny, Mary turned to look at Bernard, in whose swift emotion she felt herself being born again. Just so had she herself, thirty years ago, exulted in the marvel and the beauty of these chicks. How many generations of the pretty senseless things had been hatched and reared, crammed and butchered, since that long dreaming summer she had spent, a child of ten, with Mrs Pusey ! But this thought did not enter Mary's mind. Seen again through a child's eyes, yet enriched with a mature emotion, the picture in which she stood had a quality self-luminous, eternal. To her imagination these were the selfsame chickens, this the selfsame kitchen, as had charmed so long ago the child she had been : through all the storm and stress of the years they had remained intact, peerless in beauty and in power to evoke the beauty in her soul, so that to cross the threshold of Jinny's cottage had been to step out of time into her own

particular corner of the kingdom of heaven,
a corner illumined, populous, vocal, with all
the bright unfledged fancies of infancy.

A shadow fell across the gleaming floor.
'Well, Jinny!' quavered Mrs Downes, from
the doorway. 'I thought I must take a peep
at you. How are you, my girl?'

Jinny bobbed a curtsey. 'It's not for the
likes of me to complain, Mrs Downes, and I'm
sure it's very good and nice of you to bother
yourself about an old woman.'

'Stuff!' said Mrs Downes genially, leaning
on her ebony stick. 'Why, you're not turned
eighty yet, my dear! If youngsters like you
start talking about being old—why, what about
me?'

'Yes,' chimed in Mary. 'Mother's eighty
four, Jinny. And has all her faculties still.
Isn't she wonderful!'

'Eighty five!' Mrs Downes corrected
her sharply. 'Eighty five, Mary, in less than
six weeks.' Deeply offended, the old lady
turned from her daughter, as from a pert
schoolgirl. 'You must come and see me,
Jinny, on my birthday. Come to tea.'

Mrs Puscy, bewildered by the honour,
stammered excuses; but Granny swept them
aside. 'I'll send a carriage to fetch you. The
twenty fifth of July. Now don't forget.'

'Very well, Mrs Downes.'

'We'll chat over old times together,' pursued the inexorable dame. 'That will be fun. And I always like to have young people about me,' she added, with twinkling malice.

Old Jinny smiled wryly. The jest hurt her dignity a little; yet she enjoyed it. 'You were always one for your joke, marm. Used to set us all in fits, I well remember.' She laughed in a silent ghostly fashion at some ancient joke overlaid by the dust of half a lifetime.

For Mary the scene held a mystery that pressed urgently upon her for interpretation. She was aware, suddenly, of a singular spiritual detachment. She was aware of her body, and with sharp surprise to find herself pent, as though by some absurd accident, in that particular and perishable form. Involuntarily she glanced down at herself, at her hands and feet, at all that was visible to her of her figure, and the question burst upon her with the effect of a revelation: What am I doing here? For one instant, whether of vision or of mistaken fancy, she felt herself to be an immortal and timeless spirit, free of the universe and at one with all things, yet attached—queerly and incredibly—to a human body known as Mary Durham. She felt, rather than thought, that

this exultation filling her as with light could
not be other than the kindliness that shone
in Granny's eyes, the genial impulse behind
Jinny's laughter, Bernard's silent rapture,
and the pulsing radiance of daylight. Even
the chickens had their part in this communion ;
even into the honeysuckle that overhung the
doorway her spirit overflowed. For a moment
only. Then, a little dazed, she came home to
Mary Durham again, and listened to the old
ladies' pleasantries.

'Say what you will,' said Jinny, obstinately
grimacing, ' I'm seventy seven near enough.'

Mrs Downes chuckled, as she led the way
back to the cab. ' I dare say you are, my dear.
But you've a long way to go to catch me up.'
Consciously superior by eight years, she
climbed into the cab, followed by her family.
The two ancients smiled at each other, cantankerous and affectionate. All waved farewells ; but as the cab began moving away
Mary felt a tug at her sleeve. She looked
down into the pleading eyes of Bernard.

'What is it, dear ? '

'Mother, I *would* like a chicken for my
own.'

Swiftly, scarce able to meet that gaze, Mary
considered the plea. ' It would be lonely all
by itself,' she parried. ' No one to play with,

and no mother to take care of it. You wouldn't like that, would you?' It was in her mind that such fragile prettiness must not be put to the test of personal possession. 'Besides, they belong to Mrs Pusey, all those chicks.'

'Couldn't you buy me one?' persisted Bernard.

'I know what we'll do, Bernard. We'll come to look at them another day, shall we? And perhaps see whether Mrs Pusey will part with one.'

'Oo, yes!' said Bernard. His joy was complete. He smiled gravely, in unalloyed happiness; and Mary smiled with him. Mrs Pusey might, or might not, consent to sell one of her chickens; but the golden birds that filled Bernard's vision, making pensive his large eyes throughout that homeward journey: these could never be bought or sold.

THE RENEWAL OF YOUTH

THE RENEWAL OF YOUTH

IT is a strange, a fantastic trade, said Saunders, that of the novelist. To sit at home cutting pieces off oneself, not devotionally, like a fanatical fakir, but for sale—really there is something almost indecent about it when you think of it in that way. Not that a man writes autobiography in his fiction : to suppose that (as you will be quick to tell me) is the most vulgar of errors, an error which only the unimaginative can entertain for a moment. Your novelist retails, not his personal history, but rather his personal essence, his quality, the spiritual precipitate that remains in the bottom of his test-tube when the experiment is over, remains to be subtly modified by every succeeding experiment, until the inevitable smash reduces all his brave dreams and discoveries to a handful of dust and broken glass. But death is not the only obliterator of records and of the quintessential wisdom into which the mind of an artist is able to condense records. There is another path to oblivion. The enemy of life is able to achieve the same effect by a gesture more delicate, more ironical, working havoc in a man under the guise of renewing his youth. This is what happened to my old friend Humphrey Dyke Smith, as you shall hear.

I call him my friend, as indeed he was ; but long years ago I had delighted to express my homage by calling him master. Youth, especially idealistic youth aspiring to literature, can use this language without feeling absurd. Certainly I did not feel absurd when I first stood, a boy of eighteen, in the presence of my hero. You can imagine my sensations ; none better. I glowed with exultation, I blushed with embarrassment and a sense of my own unworthiness, to find myself confronting an admittedly great novelist. I need not relate now the circumstances that had made me dare to send to Humphrey Dyke (for so, as you know, he appeared on his title-pages) a handful of my own jejune and juvenile fiction. Suffice it that I *had* sent it, and that he, with the unassuming kindliness of the very great, had invited me to call and ' have a chat ' about the stuff. I dare say I had my share of auctorial vanity in those days ; but, even then, the last thing I wished to discuss with this king among lions was the literary activity of myself, the most humble of mice. Nor did we in fact spend much time on that unprofitable subject. He gave me generous encouragement, far more than my work deserved or my subsequent performances justified ; and then he took me to see his roses. It enhanced his charm for me to find that he seemed readier to discourse on the lethal efficacy of quassia-chips than on literature. In appearance the man was as robust, masculine and distinguished as his own books.

He was then at the zenith of his fame, and indeed of his achievement. Yet he continued, for nearly two decades, to produce work which, though it did not surpass his previous best, was not inferior to it either in inspirational power or delicacy of execution. During those years it was my privilege to visit him frequently. At our first meeting there had been but fifteen years between us, and these, as I matured, seemed to dwindle away to almost nothing. In fundamental brain-power there was always, of course, an enormous disparity between us, for Dyke, though he developed comparatively late, was a man of intellect as well as a man of genius. But even this disparity was soon lost to view : Dyke himself saw to that. Quite contentedly he kept his conversation within my intellectual compass, and yet contrived to get some pleasure from my company. In the season we played a great deal of tennis together on his private courts ; in the winter we played chess. Sometimes, too, we had long and for me fascinating conferences about his work ; but those I must tell you more about some other time, for they do not belong to this story. Very soon I reached the wise conclusion that I was more fitted to talk about literature than to produce it. I gave up my own scribbling and took to theology, abandoning one form of fiction for another, you will say. But though I ceased wooing the Muse I was always ready to play Pandarus to another's wooing. All my life I have been a haunter of literary salons— by which I mean that where two or three writers are gathered together, there am I in the midst. That will partly explain to you my predilection for your own ungodly society.

It was in my curate days that my friendship with Dyke took root. After I came to this living we saw a good deal less of each other for a while, until, at the death of his widowed mother, he sold up his home and came to live within four miles of me in the pleasant country house you know well. No doubt you have made at least one pious pilgrimage to it. A whitewashed, red-roofed house, with leaded casement windows and a front door in heavy black oak rather ecclesiastical in appearance. In the front, tall pines ; at the back, roses growing in a little grove of silver birches planted by Dyke himself five years ago. Of conventional carpet-gardening there is none. The place is something of a wilderness, and he loved it to be so. It was in this house, eighteen months ago, that the mysterious catastrophe occurred which at one strike restored him to health and happiness and deprived modern letters of a writer who, in the opinion of many, was second only to Thomas Hardy.

Restored him, I say ; for he had been ailing for many months, and the sombre philosophy that characterises all his books began to degenerate into a personal and despairing pessimism. He had fallen out of love with life. The death of his wife had soured rather than broken him ; for he now spent a deplorable proportion of his time making public gestures of contempt at the universe, shaking his fist, so to speak, at God. Hardy, at his bitterest, is less savage than was Dyke in some of these diatribes, many of which were never printed. 'If only he could contrive to forget his loss,' we said to ourselves who watched him grow daily more gaunt, more aged. No doubt his general bodily weakness was due to nervous disorder, and that in its turn must have been due, in large measure, to his new habit of mind, his angry brooding upon the series of indignities to which man is subjected in this mortal life. He had lost poise. Yet not wholly, for even during that dark and ever darkening period he was busy upon a novel, his last, which reveals, in spite of its unparalleled savagery, no falling off in literary power. You've read it, of course —*The Inviolable Shade*, a trite silly title chosen by Dyke's publishers after the catastrophe to which I have referred. You agree that it is not the least of his works.

One morning he woke, after a night of profound sleep, with all his physical ailments forgotten. Alas, it was not only those he had forgotten. Bateson, his aged manservant, came into his room to draw the curtains. Bateson, you must know, had been in the family from boyhood.

' It is a beautiful morning, sir,' remarked Bateson, as he let the sunshine into the room. ' The birds are singing in the garden, sir, in a way that one would scarcely credit.' I have it on Bateson's own authority that this is precisely what he said. I gathered that he was in the habit of opening the day with some little observation such as this. It was his contribution to the task of inducing serenity in his master.

On this occasion Dyke's reception of the matutinal homily was unusual. 'Cheerio, dad!' he called, boisterously flinging aside the bedclothes.

'Ha, ha, sir!' Bateson laughed, as in duty bound. 'Very good, I'm sure, sir. As if the likes of me could be the father of a gentleman. A very laughable fancy indeed, sir.'

'I'm glad you approve of my little pleasantry, Bateson. But—hell, where am I?'

'Where *are* you, sir?' Bateson stared. 'I don't think I understand you.'

'Where am I?' cried Dyke again, a boyish ring in his voice. 'This room is deuced strange to me.' He stared at Bateson, awaiting an explanation. 'Have you been up to some lark, Bateson? ... My sainted aunt!—what's come over you, man?'

'I'm not aware,' said Bateson, a little stiffly, 'that anything's overcome me, sir. As for playing tricks: at my age....'

'But, my dear fellow,' Dyke protested, 'you look thirty years older than you did last night!'

'Time tells on us all, sir. One don't always care to be reminded, if I may make the observation.'

'Now look here, Bateson, be a sport. Tell

me, did I get home late last night? Carrying a pretty heavy cargo, eh?'

'You didn't go out at all yesterday, sir. And if it's liquor you're allooding to, if you took as much as two glasses of sherry, that's all you did take, and not so much as a thimbleful more, sir.'

Dyke winked. 'You're a treasure, Bateson. Tell the same tale to the old lady, and all's well.'

'If you're referring to Mrs Bateson, sir. . . .'

'I'm not, my dear chap. I'm referring to my sainted mother.'

At last even Bateson began to understand. 'God bless my soul, you don't mean to say . . . Don't you remember, sir, that your mother, poor lady, is . . . gone aloft, as the poet says, sir?'

Dyke sat on the bed pulling his trousers on. He looked up resentfully at Bateson's words. 'Damn it, Bateson, don't you know better than to take advantage of a gentleman when he's got a thick head! The joke's in bad taste. You'd better run off to your duties.'

'Very good, sir.'

Bateson, his wits in a whirl, walked from the room with as much dignity as he could command. He was recalled by a yell that set his nerves quivering. Trembling in every muscle, the poor old man rushed panting up the stairs again, and, after a paralysed moment of sheer terror, re-entered the room from which he had just been dismissed. He found his master staring, with wild eyes that burned like cinders in his livid face, into the wardrobe mirror. He turned that terrible face to Bateson.

' I'm grey,' he confided, in a hoarse whisper. ' My skin's all lined. It wasn't like that yesterday, Bateson. My Christ, am I going mad ? '

Tears rolled down the old servant's cheeks. ' I'm sure I hope not sir,' he answered, invincibly respectful. ' And in any case it wouldn't become me to say——'

Dyke clutched the man's arm viciously. ' Tell me, for God's sake, *am* I grey ? Look at me and tell the truth before I strangle you ! '

' Your hair is greying, sir, without a doubt.'

' Ah ! And my skin, dry and wrinkled about the eyes. *Old*, Bateson, *old* ? Is it so ? '

' Not more than one would expect in the circumstances, sir. We're none of us so young as we were. . . . You're hurting my arm, sir, if I may take the liberty.'

'Not so young as we were!' Dyke turned to the mirror again to examine the ravages time had made. 'But I'm not nineteen yet, you fool!'

'Sixty one, sir. Begging your pardon.'

To shut out the sight of himself Dyke buried his face in his hands, turned blindly about, and plunged on to the bed with the jerky spasmodic movement of a man brought down by a bullet.

'There, there!' said Bateson, patting those hunched and shaking shoulders. 'You're not quite yourself, sir. That's all. I'll get you a little pick-me-up, and all will be as merry as . . . as a marriage-bell, so to speak, sir.' He tottered from the room to invoke the assistance of his wife, Dyke's housekeeper, and of young Perkins, Dyke's confidential secretary.

2

You can imagine the scenes that followed better than I can describe them. Suppose you were to wake up to-morrow morning and find yourself to be a withered old man, and you will understand poor Dyke's state of mind. For a long while he simply could not be brought to believe the truth. He called everybody a liar without distinction of persons. But after a day or two he had to face the facts. If, as he half thought, he was merely suffering from a bad dream, he had to confess that it was a remarkably consistent dream, and apparently a continuous one, for it showed no signs of ending. He felt that he had been stripped suddenly of his youth ; that, by some devilish miracle, he had been forced to leap, in one evil night, the forty middle years of his life. One effect of this was to bring death hideously nearer to one who had had no time to school himself to the thought of that ultimate doom. He had indeed schooled himself to it, but the effects of that schooling, like everything else pertaining to the middle period, were utterly obliterated. The blank space in his memory was as clean as a slate wiped by a wet sponge. When, for the purposes of test, we mentioned his late wife to him, he was interested only as one is interested in the love-affairs of a total stranger. The women he met in the pages of light fiction—and now he read quite a deal of light fiction—were more real to him than was the woman whose death had laid waste his life not many months before. Our prayer that he might forget had been answered, and with a vengeance.

Only for a day or two did he abandon

himself to miserable forebodings. His very immaturity saved him. He set himself to study the new part he must play in the world, worked up the facts about himself methodically as though preparing for an examination. One thing he would not do ; nor did we seek to persuade him. Some obscure instinct forbade him to read his own books. Young Perkins, an able and a very sympathetic fellow, proved an admirable coach. Quick to understand his employer's altered psychology, he pretended to be serenely unaware of anything tragic in the situation. He took it all as a matter of course, and Dyke himself, after that first futile raging, accepted it with a kind of levity. 'When I go up for my Responsions, Perkins,' he would begin. And Perkins would cut in quickly, 'Pardon me, Mr Dyke, your Oxford days are over. You will remember what I told you yesterday.' Perkins had been the most passionate admirer of the great Dyke, and it was he, undoubtedly, who bore the brunt of the tragedy.

I happened to be present during one of these lesson-hours.

'If you take my advice,' Perkins was saying, as I entered the room, ' you will make a note of these things.' His air was that of a sorely tried Director of Studies. 'I will give you once again a short précis of your career. Now it was in 1885, when your second novel appeared, that you dropped using your surname. From that time onward you have been known, privately as well as professionally, as Humphrey Dyke.'

'And my first novel, what about that?'

'Your first novel bore all three names on its title-page, Humphrey Dyke Smith. Or rather, the first edition did. For this reason it is much sought after by collectors. The last copy I heard of fetched £20 at Sotheby's. The second edition, which differs from the first only in being short of the one word Smith, is worth but little more than its original price.'

'Twenty quid for five letters,' said Dyke frivolously. 'Pretty good pay, that! I must have been a fair-sized bug, Perkins?'

'You were,' said Perkins curtly.

Perkins continued to discourse, while Dyke from time to time made notes in an exercise-book that had been provided for that purpose. I idled about the room, fingering books, and pretending to read a paragraph here and there. Presently out of the tail of my eye I saw Dyke pause in his writing and look up at Perkins. There was something in his glance that made me bite my lips in pain. 'It's rather fun, isn't it, Perkins?' he said, boyishly wistful.

'Very amusing indeed,' answered Perkins in a rather loud harsh voice. And he jumped up from his chair and ran from the room with puckered face.

3

I persuaded Dyke to pay me a visit now and again, always hoping that another miracle might undo the evil wrought by the first one, and so restore my old friend to me. Our first meeting, after his lapse of memory, had been painful, naturally. We were re-introduced by Perkins, who, with that correct official air he now affected, explained carefully who and what I was. Gradually we became acquainted. Dyke, now a mere boy, treated me with a mixture of deference and banter that I should have found charming in a man really young. I remember he called once while I was correcting the proofs of *The Inviolable Shade*, a task I had gladly undertaken in order to relieve the devoted Perkins of a painful duty.

'Proof-sheets,' cried Dyke, seizing upon them with glee. 'How exciting! May I look? . . . By Jove, that was awfully rude of me, wasn't it, to grab them like that!

Do you mind me having a peep, Mr Saunders?'

While I hesitated he took my permission for granted. And I, on reflection, encouraged him to read on.

'Oh, it's a novel. Thought it was your sermons, don't you know.' He dropped into a chair, and read for five minutes. 'Is it your own work, Mr Saunders?' How it hurt me to be called Mr Saunders!

I answered that the author was a friend of mine.

'Bit over my head, I'm afraid,' Dyke said cheerfully. 'Don't quite see what your friend is getting at.'

Before I had an answer ready he blushed self-consciously and began fumbling in his pocket. 'That reminds me. I've been trying my hand at writing, and I should value your opinion if you'll be so good. You're a tremendous reader, I know.'

He handed me his manuscript. My fingers trembled as they closed upon it. A faint hope stirred in me.

'It's a poem,' explained Dyke, 'and it's about a . . . well, some one I met the other day in the village.'

I remember a few lines of that poem. Indeed I can't forget them.

> Her eyes are heavenly blue; her hair falls down
> In gleaming ringlets like a golden crown.
> Looking at me from under lashes long,
> Her mystic beauty moves me like a song.

This from a man who had narrowly missed the Nobel Prize! I was bereft of speech.

'I'll tell you all about her some day,' promised Dyke, misinterpreting my silence. 'At present I'm too frightfully happy. She's really a wonderful inspiration. I sometimes think that she'll be the means of my getting back my . . . well, my literary powers, you know. Perkins is a bit doubtful about it, but he's an awful old raven. Do you think there's a chance, sir?'

I handed him back his manuscript, but I could not bear to look upon the wistful hope that trembled in his eyes. 'Well, it's a start, isn't it?' I said weakly.

His face lit up. 'Do you really think so? That's one in the eye for old Perkins, anyhow!'

**

Saunders broke off abruptly. For three or four minutes he stared reflectively into the fire. At last I ventured my protest.

'But that's not the end, Saunders! You can't stop there.'

'Indeed, it *is* the end,' Saunders answered.

'From that day until his death, ten years later, Dyke lived in a state of adolescent happiness, enhanced and interrupted, as adolescent happiness always is, by the ecstasies and agonies of a series of love-affairs. He lived in a fool's paradise—the only paradise any of us can hope to attain, this side the grave.'

SUMMERS END

SUMMERS END

AS for getting up early, Harriet would promise anything in the world if thereby she might have the adventure of riding with her uncle in a bumping wagon over the dim white roads and through the tingling air of morning.

'Ever so early I'll be ready,' said Harriet, at the tea-table, 'if only you'll wake me up, uncle. As early as early as early can be!'

Uncle Bob barked brief laughter, shaking his beard in the process, and screwing up his greenish eyes until they resembled the little rayed suns of the picture-book. Uncle Bob's eyes were at once fierce and kindly. He was broad and big and squat. His whiskers were so prodigious that they scarcely left room for the more personal features: like an abundant forest growing in red soil they flourished on chin and cheek and neck. Even from the broad nostrils they sprouted, though certainly with less decision. He was quite the hairiest man Harriet, at seven, had ever seen, and very nearly the nicest. He had a good crop of stories—rather terrible, earthy stories—though being merely human he could not compete with Harriet's father in this respect. He was rather like a huge friendly dog or a well-disposed bear: always ready in his leisure to romp and roar (indeed, his very speech was a roar), always smelling pleasantly of pigs or cowsheds. He was, in fact, the living symbol or epitome of Summers End in its homelier aspects: in him the farm—or at least the farmyard—had become flesh. He wore breeches and gaiters and fascinating leather cuffs attached to his sleeves. His clothes were the colour of the stale mustard that Harriet was accustomed to see in the cruet at home; and his neck, exposed by an open shirt, was brick-red. He was the wildest man, as well as the hairiest, and he inspired Harriet not only with affection but with a delicious fear. There was always the remote chance, too remote to be a source of positive terror, that he might one day grow extra hungry and eat her all up.

'What!' shouted Uncle Bob, when his mirth had found adequate vent. 'Be up at ha' past four, would you?' From the tone and volume of his voice he might have been addressing the most recalcitrant of his carthorses. ' Ha' past four, *heigh* ? '

' Oo yes,' cried Harriet. ' As early as early as early can be,' she chanted again.

Uncle Bob laughed once more. An easily amused man, Uncle Bob. ' Earlyish for little gals, me dear ! Well, well, well ! '

He hastened to fill his mouth with an incredible bite from a doorstep of bread-and-jam, pausing in mastication, a moment later, to pour a cupful of dark brown tea into that same accommodating cavity. He munched with energy, deftly reclaimed from his moustache some strayed particles both liquid and solid, and pushed back his chair. ' Now then, Bert me boy ! '

Bert, grunting acquiescence, helped himself to a slab of cake, and took no notice of his father's stamping across the room. At the door the older man turned his head. ' Milking,' said father. ' Ay,' replied son. The monosyllable struggled for utterance through a mouthful of cake.

Harriet liked Cousin Bert, if only because he too was part of Summers End and was invested with something of its glamour. She would perhaps have loved him had he been a shade less sulky. He seemed, she had to confess, sadly lacking in appreciation of the beautiful things and enchanting people by which he was surrounded. Harriet was not so absorbed in her sensations as to have no thought to spare for her friends, and she was quick to detect that Cousin Bert was not entirely at peace with his world. He had something on his mind. How else account for his long silences, his avoidance of Aunt Polly's searching glances, his failure to join in Uncle Bob's jollity, and his amazing indifference to all the happiness that pervaded Summers End like a smell ?—imperfect simile, for the smell itself was happiness, and happiness itself the fusion of sight and sound and smell. Not that Harriet worked the problem out, collecting evidence of Bert's disgruntlement and drawing a logical inference. No : she simply felt the discord in him and was timidly sorry about it. It was as definite and as unknown a quantity as would be a solid obstacle run into in the dark. Yet even Cousin Bert, infected by her new delight in the world, sometimes for brief spells emerged from the mysterious dream that commonly enveloped him. He had shewn her the caged rabbits, being fattened for what purpose she knew not ; had dug for her in the garden an elaborate system of canals, watered by the pump through rubber tubing ; had instructed her in the art of spoon-feeding with worms the hens that clucked and scratched behind their wire-netting. Not perhaps a very pretty game, this last. It was conceivable that the worms did not enjoy it. But worms were such nasty things, and hens so lovely, that it was surely legitimate to please the one at the expense of the other, especially if one happened to please oneself at the same time. Cousin Bert, anyhow, made short work of her doubts. Yet she was conscious that his heart was neither in this nor in any of the other amusements he devised, from time to time, for her benefit. His interest in them manifestly lacked sincerity. A strange man, this Cousin Bert ; a problem, indeed, though not an urgent one. Despite his great age—he approached twenty two—Harriet felt maternally towards him. Bert, however, was already provided with a mother, known to his little cousin as Aunt Polly ; and to mask his preoccupation from the watchful eyes of this mother was now his constant care. A sure instinct urged him to this secrecy : he knew that his mother was wise enough to understand his situation, but not young enough to enter into it imaginatively. He would not have expressed his conviction so, for it had become his habit to express himself mainly in grunts and growls and stubborn action ; but there the conviction was, at the bottom of his inarticulate soul. He was locked in the loneliness of adolescence.

'Now, darling,' said Aunt Polly to Harriet, 'finish up your tea.'

Promptly Harriet removed her interested stare from her cousin's face, and began dabbing up the crumbs on her plate with a moistened forefinger. 'No, Harriet : that's not the way. Eat nicely. Please do.' Aunt Polly had a way with her that made one want to please her at whatever cost to one's own convenience. She made it a personal matter rather than one of discipline. She did not refer one to an ideal standard of behaviour : she appealed to one's compassion for her feelings. At once, with no interval of hesitation or disappointment, Harriet began eating 'nicely,' so anxious was she to oblige her beloved aunt. If Uncle Bob was the symbol of the farmyard, Aunt Polly was as certainly the cool, clean, delightful dairy made manifest. She was as plump as butter, as mild as milk ; she was placid and comfortable and infinitely kind ; and she had scarcely more outward animation than one of her own cows.

'And after tea,' said Aunt Polly, 'shall we do a little sewing together, you and I ? '

Harriet assented the more readily to this

proposal, which did not greatly attract her, because she had, as she thought, already won her point with Uncle Bob. She was to ride with him, in those hours of the morning which she had never before experienced, to fetch a load of swedes for the cattle. She knew that there might be earwigs in the wagon, but that was a possibility one must face boldly. She need not, after all, sit down : more fun, indeed, to stand and sway, precariously balanced, with one eye on the lolloping old mare and one on the diminishing yet continuing ribbon of road, the pearly grey sky, the smooth-gliding and fragrant hedges. Already she seemed to feel the cart jolting under her, to hear the metallic patter of the shod hooves' contact with the ground, to see the broad haunch and the swishing tail and the sharp equine ears moving up and down in front of her. Already, little freshets of keen air, like fairy whips, stung sharp colour into her cheeks. What mattered earwigs ? Nasty though the creatures were, their dangerousness was over-rated. Once an earwig had crept down her neck and secreted himself under her camisole. A shocking experience, fully justifying her passionate screams. Yet she had survived it, and could survive it again. She braced herself for the perilous adventure, well content to be sojourning in a world of which even the terrors did but add a flavour, a queer zest, to the all-pervading jolliness.

2

Soon after Harriet had gone to bed Bert Growcock returned from his final round of farm duties to find his mother awaiting him. She was knitting busily and gave no sign of having noticed his entry, but he was not deceived. Sensitive to atmosphere in spite of his dull looks, he was aware at once that she was lying in wait for him ; and she, from whom he perhaps had inherited his sensitiveness, was instantly aware of his awareness. He knew that she sought to invade his solitude ; she knew that he would resist the invasion. No word was said, but the air of the kitchen was quick with the clash of their wills. He picked up the local paper from the table, on which a light supper was already set out, and sat down opposite her in a creaking basket chair. The lamp shed a soft yellow glow in the room. The hearth was kindled, warm. On the varnished mantelpiece a cheap marble clock, picked up at a recent sale, monotonously ticked their lives away. The mother bided her time. The son, uneasy, shifted in his seat.

'Well,' remarked Bert, running his eye down his news sheet, ' I suppose old Pappin's dead at last.'

' I suppose so,' assented Mrs Growcock.

There was nothing at all suppositional about their belief in Pappin's death. They were employing a local turn of speech. The famous Pappin, full of years, was indubitably dead and buried, as the newspaper testified with much loquacity.

' Nice to see a bit of fire,' observed Bert, after a longer silence.

' Yes. Summer's over before it's begun, this year. Never needed fires in September when I was a young woman. As Mrs Foster was saying only yesterday, the summer gets shorter every year.'

Mrs Growcock quoted this remark only to comfort herself, knowing in her heart that it was untrue, and wishing by repetition to make it sound true. For what was happening had nothing to do with the seasons. Not in the stars, but in her blood, was the cause of this premature chilliness. She was no longer a young woman ; every day her grasp on middle-age became more tenuous ; and lately she had taken to thinking about herself and had found the process painful. She was aware of having worked very hard for a great number of years, worked and suffered and remained obstinately cheerful, paying dearly for every fugitive pleasure ; and now, with a husband who took life too easily, and a son who took it too hard, she was constrained to wonder if anything had been worth while. If Bert, her only achievement, Bert, for whose life she had paid in blood and tears and toil and incessant prayerfulness—if he, too, missed happiness, she was cheated of all satisfaction, the dupe of nature and of hope.

' Rain about to-night,' said Bert, ' shouldn't wonder.'

' . . . twenty four, twenty five,' counted Mrs Growcock, casting off her stitches. ' When are you thinking of getting married, Bert ? '

But she did not in the least take him by surprise. He had been momently expecting, if not just this, something equally uncompromising.

' No hurry for that,' he returned easily. ' Hardly old enough, am I ? '

' No, but you're young enough,' said his mother shrewdly. ' What does *she* think about it, my boy ? '

No match for her as a fencer, he was caught off his guard. ' What, Lottie ? ' he said eagerly. And frowned, realising his blunder,

Mrs Growcock's black bone knitting needles clattered on the tiled floor. When she had recovered them her face was flushed with the exertion of stooping. 'Ay,' she said, and her voice lacked its accustomed steadiness. 'What does Lottie Marsh say about it?'

'May be she's waiting till she's asked,' suggested Bert. But his cunning was a minute too late. 'Of course,' he said, temper rising, 'if you've been poking round, mother, there's no more to be said.' Shrugging his shoulders he made a great show of unfolding again the paper he had discarded.

'I haven't deserved that,' she answered. Her face was unnaturally pale, her voice dispassionate. 'A mother doesn't need to go poking round. May be I've no right to know your affairs, but when I see you making yourself miserable I use my eyes, that's all. Why not tell me about it and have done?'

Seeing the emotion that she strove to conceal, and mistaking its cause, the boy was stung to compunction. 'Sorry, mum,' he said, reverting to a schoolboy habit. 'I don't mind you knowing. But it's not easy to talk. If I married her the governor would be certain to make hell about it. The daughter of his own shepherd, of all people. I know these self-made men.'

'Don't bring your father into it,' she advised him coldly. 'Self-made or not, he may have good reason for opposing such a marriage.'

'What reason?'

Mrs Growcock countered his question with one of her own. 'Don't you know what they say of her?'

'What do they say?' he asked.

'Well, for one thing, she's illegitimate. Did you know that?'

Bert's face clouded, but lightened almost at once. 'So that's it, is it? All this fuss because Lottie's father wasn't married to her mother. That stuff's out of date, mum. I know what I must do. I must get out of this and take a decent job. After all, I wasn't educated for farming.'

'Farming paid for your education,' she reminded him.

The talk was degenerating into a squabble, and both seemed powerless to arrest the degeneration. The son retired once more behind his paper; the mother resumed her knitting. But still his eyes scowled; and hers, staring absently at her work, were glazed with a vision of tragedy. 'Are you very fond of her?' she asked softly, not looking up.

He grunted an embarrassed affirmative.

' How far has it gone ? '

' Far enough.' His voice choked. ' There's no going back now, thank God ! '

At that she looked up. ' No ! ' she cried sharply. ' Put the paper down, Bert, and listen to me. You must forget this girl, do you understand ? '

He answered curtly, behind his paper : ' I understand nothing of the sort. I shall marry her.'

Her face was blanched with pain. Was this to be the bitter fruit of her long maternal labour, the carrying, the giving birth, the endless anxious vigilance ? Was this the purpose of life, this crucifixion of the spirit ? But, though she winced at her own agony, self-pity was lost in a larger and purer compassion. And in her deepest heart she found, as an ultimate refuge, pride like a rock. She was strong in despair. Life, whatever bitter turn it took, was a challenge that she scorned to decline : what it inflicted she would silently and disdainfully endure. But the heroic moment dwindled away.

' My darling boy,' she began. A sound outside caught her attention, and the weakness in her snatched at the excuse. The door was flung open ; her husband stood swaying in the doorway. ' Oh, Bob,' she said, ' do come in. I want you to have a talk with Bert. We're in trouble.'

But Bob Growcock was not in talkative mood. With an unmeaning grin, which passed instantly, he lurched towards the table and fell into a chair. In a few seconds he was asleep and snoring, with his head in a plate of bread-and-butter.

His son eyed him sardonically. 'What price fetching swedes in the morning? I'll arrange the gentleman for bed, mother. You be off!'

He went to shut the door his father had left open. He stepped out into the night, elaborately unconcerned and stubborn. A thousand stars struggled through mist. The moon was veiled in a menace that the grey wind voiced.

He stepped back into the house, shut and bolted the door, and returned to the kitchen, which his mother was just leaving. 'Good night, mum,' he said, lightly kissing her forehead. 'Dirty weather to-morrow, shouldn't wonder.'

3

Harriet went to bed, to dream but not to sleep, or so it seemed to her. She did in fact sleep a trifle of eight hours or so, but opening her eyes in the darkness some long while before dawn she felt that she had been awake all the time, so faithful had been her dreams to the glory that morning was to bring. She was alone in the room. At Summers End, indeed, she was altogether alone, her parents and her two mature sisters being still at home. It was part of the charm of Summers End that she did not belong to it. With Uncle Bob and Aunt Polly she was conscious of no sort of blood-relationship : they were foreigners, strange and exciting in everything they did. Nobody troubled her with the information that Aunt Polly was her father's eldest sister who had made an indiscreet runaway match with a social inferior ; nor would it have been credible to her that her father could possess a sister. Anyhow, an aunt is an aunt, and cannot be a sister as well. In Harriet's world uncles and aunts were as common as blackberries ; every one who became intimate with her family was endowed with one or another of these titles, which consequently had no definite meaning for her.

Long before it was light she stole out of bed to peep through the window at a world mysteriously dim and still. Bert's prediction had been in part fulfilled ; but the storm was now spent and all the dark shapes outside were touched with cold silver. It slanted across the gables of the clustering outbuildings, flung a large, clear triangle on the stable door, picked out the near side of a gate-post, and settled, like quivering tinsel, on the nose and forepaws of the hugest dog in the world. At sight of this beast Harriet could not repress a gasp. He seemed to be staring with the most sinister intention straight up at her window. She drew back into the shadow of the room, only to find the object of her terror resolve itself, under long scrutiny, into a tall bush. A sloping field beyond, its surface broken by a solitary haystack, lay as if tranced in sleep under a shimmering diaphane of moonlight. Surely it must soon be time for her to get up and go out with Uncle Bob into that region of pale dream! As she stood there, gazing out, gradually the wonder of the waning night subdued her urgent desire, so that she forgot it and was content to float out on the wings of imagination and dip her spirit in the dove-grey, luminous ocean. Night paled under her stare.

The sudden apparition of a man in the yard below, not unlike her uncle, startled her to a realisation of her vigil's purpose. The man led out a horse and cart. He strode across the yard—no mistaking that walk—and opened the gate that gave on to the road. Tears rose to Harriet's watching and incredulous eyes. Torn with grief by her disappointment, she was affected even more profoundly by this vision of human infidelity. The stability of her world was shaken, and she was afraid with a fear that had never entered her heart before. When the rumbling of the wagon had died away she turned back, emptied of hope, to her bed. She felt herself deserted, forgotten, alone in a dark and alien universe.

In the morning, renewed by a subsequent sleep, she reduced Aunt Polly to confusion by an abrupt question. Even Bert paused in his breakfasting, surprised by the chill maturity of the child's tone. 'Why did Uncle Bob go without me this morning?'

'He must have forgotten,' said Aunt Polly.

'I see.'

Harriet's grave acceptance of the explanation was more eloquent than tears. Her simple affirmation seemed weighted with a significance of which she herself was unaware. It was as if she did indeed see, in clear-eyed despair, the incurable fickleness of mankind. It was as if sin and death suddenly confronted her. Bert, already tight-strung with suppressed emotion, could not bear to witness the change in her. 'I tell you what,' he impulsively said. 'You come with me to the station with the milk. That'll be fun, eh?'

Harriet, with her new sad wisdom, was half afraid to rejoice in this glorious prospect. 'Ride in the cart with the milk-cans!' she said, unable now to believe in such happiness.

'With the churns. Yes. Come along, or we'll miss the train.'

Bert blushed, already, for reasons of his own, regretting his kindly impulse; and, ashamed of his regret yet unable to stifle it, he made shift to avoid looking at his cousin as she ran out with him into the yard. For her the world was born again in splendour. She forgot her sadness and her brooding fears. Life once more was friendly, caressing; and the fallen sons of men were reinvested with the attributes of deity. She stood first on one leg, then on the other, twisting her slim body from side to side, unable to rest; unable, in her impatience, to take her usual delight in all the details of harnessing the grey pony; unable to fire at Bert the customary round of excited questions about this and that. If life held a purer joy than riding in a cart in the company of huge milk-churns, she was powerless to conceive it.

At last they were off. The road was slipping away under the turning wheels. The churns were rattling, and the milk in them audibly splashing. It was evident now to Harriet that she had been making a grave mistake about Bert. He, and not Uncle Bob, was the nicest person in the world. His gentleness when he lifted her into the cart, his queer shy smile : everything pointed to the same conclusion. When she grew up she would come to live with Cousin Bert for ever and ever.

'We'll stop here for a minute,' said Bert, pulling up. 'Just have a look on the floor, Harriet, to see if there are any earwigs about.' Harriet had advertised her opinion of earwigs. 'I won't be long.'

Obligingly Harriet made a systematic search. It was soon completed. She stood up to make her report. Where was Bert? 'Cousin Bert-ee!' she called. But he was only a few yards away, in intimate talk with a young woman. Harriet caught sight of the pair just as they were making their farewells. The sight had no significance for her, and it was important that Bert's mind should be set at rest about the earwigs.

'There isn't any earwigs,' cried Harriet. 'Not even a little one.'

Bert returned to her. His blush and his shining eyes, whatever their cause, made him look pleasanter than ever. 'Is that your sister?' asked Harriet, in whose mind sisters and kisses were closely associated.

'Not exactly,' mumbled Bert, with a smile. 'Come, off we go again!'

But before the reluctant pony had decided to respond to his *clk-clk*, Bert became aware that an approaching wagon had stopped three yards ahead of him, and that in the wagon sat his father, regarding him from under black brows.

'Ho! ho!' roared Bob Growcock, suddenly assaulting the silence. 'So that's the cause of your mopes, is it! That's why you wear a face like a thunderstorm! Bit o' wenching, *heigh*?'

Bert paled; the reins trembled in his hand. 'Better mind what you're saying, father,' he said in a low tone.

'Mind what I'm saying, heigh? Ho, that's a good 'un. That's a real good 'un.' The greenish eyes were screwed up in a kind of mirth, but Harriet no longer took pleasure in the spectacle. Her own eyes grew rounder and more frightened as she stared at this strange Uncle Bob. The man's mirth subsided abruptly. When he spoke again his voice had a new quality. 'Well, who's the woman, lad?'

The question was peremptory, and the young man resented it. 'That's my business.'

'So 'tis,' said Growcock, with irony. 'Well, I never did! Now if I might be guessing, she come out of yonder cottage, heigh?'

Bert's sullen silence answered him.

'I thought so.' The man spat on his hands, and rubbed them together joyfully. 'And that's Marsh's cottage. And the girl was young Lottie, heigh?'

'What if it was?' said Bert angrily. 'I'm driving on.'

Bob Growcock lifted his arms and suddenly bellowed with laughter. His mirth was gargantuan. His heavy frame shook, and his eyes dwindled to nothing. Bert stared in disgust, Harriet in rising fear. 'By glory!' gasped the wild man, when he had gained some little control of himself, 'that's the best joke I ever did hear. Good boy, good boy! Keeping it in the family, heigh?'

'What do you mean?' Bert's voice made Harriet turn to look into his face. She herself was trying to laugh, and wondering why Bert did not share in the joke.

'Ah, sonny, you don't know, do ye? Your fine schooling hasn't taught you everything. A rare fool I've got for a son. Lottie Marsh —that's a good 'un. Me own little girl!

And you, you great booby . . . !' He gathered up the reins. 'Son and darter, son and darter. It's a prime one.'

Bert, with a jungle cry, slashed wildly out with the butt of his whip. His father's obscene laughter poisoned the sunlight. The whip fell harmlessly against the back of the other cart, which was already in motion. Diminishing peals of merriment continued to reach the boy's ears. His distracted glance fell on Harriet, who cowered white-faced in a corner, her arms hugging a churn as though it had power to comfort her. The sight shocked him back to his senses. Tenderness, reborn, overwhelmed him, bringing shame in its train. 'Poor little dear!' he said, taking the child into his arms. 'Did we frighten you?'

Harriet, understanding nothing but that he was no longer angry, quickly recovered; and at sight of her recovery, released from his duty, he abandoned himself to grief. He bowed his head and hid his face. For a long while he remained so, watched by the bewildered child. Harriet began to get weary of doing nothing, and so viewed with some relief the unexpected return of the strange young woman.

'Cousin Bert! Wake up, Cousin Bert! Here's the lady coming back.'

SUMMERS END

He uncovered his face ; seized the reins.

Harriet's mind reverted to her former question, which she remembered was still unanswered. 'Is that lady your sister, Cousin Bert ? ' she asked again.

Bert Growcock raised his whip and administered a sharp cut to the dilatory and aged pony, who, surprised by this unwonted indignity, plunged forward. She trotted briskly, wondering what alien hand held her reins. The wheels flew round ; the milk-churns rattled ; and everything was jolly again.

LAST DAYS OF BINNACLE

LAST DAYS OF BINNACLE

MR PERCY BINNACLE, at the age of forty five, was a moderately prosperous bank official, a man of settled habits and unalterable views. To the twins, his daughters, and to those of his colleagues who had known him no more than a decade, he seemed to be a finished specimen of his type, the ordinary city man made perfect. Curtis, the chief cashier, who had literary habits, professed to find in Mr Binnacle the timeless quality of a character in fiction, albeit a dull character, professed to believe that he had been created, not by the usual tedious process, but by a stroke of some ironist's pen. Mr Binnacle himself would have deplored the fancy, had anybody had the daring to suggest it to him ; for he knew, as you and I know, that fancies have little or no market value. Not by imagination, but by arithmetic, are ledgers balanced and bills discounted ; the regularity of an endorsement is determined by fixed rules that are the reverse of frivolous.

Whatever others might pretend to believe of him, Mr Binnacle himself knew that he was a plain man with no nonsense about him. As a loyal servant of the bank, he disdained the fanciful ; as a strict churchman he repudiated the supernatural. That is perhaps why he was among the last to understand the nature of the strange accident that befell him, one morning, on the way to his office in Lombard Street.

In spite of the many changes wrought upon body and mind during forty five years, in one characteristic Mr Binnacle had never changed. The conservatism so marked in babyhood had survived into his middle-age ; his hatred of the unusual burned with as clear a flame as when, earlier in his career, he had had to suffer the indignity of being fed out of an inanimate bottle instead of a breathing one. The scream with which he had greeted that innovation was the first of his many public protests against Newfangled Notions. It had been a long warfare gallantly waged, and hopeless from the outset. The issue was never in doubt. Mr Binnacle was fighting against impossible odds ; the forces of change were ultimately irresistible. Not only his body and his mind, but even his clothes, which were so to speak the very essence of his personality, had been modified by the meddling fingers of Time. For Mr Binnacle had been born naked, I regret to say; not attired in the silk hat, morning coat, striped trousering, spats, and glacé kid shoes, in which we now see him hurrying to the platform of Tottenham Court Road underground station.

Mr Binnacle hurried on all business occasions; he would have considered it unseemly to do otherwise. But this morning his hurry was extreme, the outcome of a pressing need rather than of a general philosophy. Ever since his unwontedly reluctant rising, things had gone awry. Breakfast had been delayed; one of his shoelaces had snapped; and the eight seventeen from his suburban station had gone without him, a thing that had not occurred for several years. Mr Binnacle had stared at the hind parts of that train reproachfully, as though watching the departure of an unfaithful lover. With irritation tempered by a sense of bereavement he danced up and down the platform waiting for the next. In the railway coach he had fretted and fumed. And here he was, at Tottenham Court Road, determined not to endure another moment's delay.

His round shaven face, babyishly innocent,

was flushed with his exertions and perspiring freely. The knuckles of the hand that grasped his neatly rolled umbrella shone like polished ivory. Every eyelash of him, every curling finger, every vein that throbbed in his temples, expressed, to the seeing eye, an invincible resolve to catch the first train out or die in the desperate attempt. And a desperate attempt it proved. The ominous STAND CLEAR flashed into view. The great mechanical gates squealed out their warning as they moved inexorably together. The crowds that stood between Mr Binnacle and his heart's desire began backing upon him. A frenzy seized the little banker. The heroic blood of the Binnacles boiled within him. Was a lifelong record for punctuality to be marred by the trivial accident of a broken shoelace? Was he to be shut out of the paradise of his daily routine by this soulless contrivance, this thing of iron, this piece of detestable modern gimcrackery? Mr Binnacle would have respected a uniformed official. Bidden by such a one to stand back, he would have obeyed, his orderly soul rejoicing in his martyrdom even while deploring its consequences. He had no patience with people who smoke in lifts; he was brimful of indignation whenever he saw a passenger put his feet on the seat of a railway carriage. But a mere illuminated sign, a mechanical siren, a wretched pair of automatic gates—for these he had nothing but dislike and contempt. By them he would not be denied admittance.

With incredible ferocity and lightning speed he elbowed his way through the crowd, ignoring the protests of a pale young man in spectacles, deaf to the scream of the plump woman with a bundle who, obstructing his passage at the last moment, had to be butted violently aside. It was for all the world as though he were back at his secondary school playing football. An indignant masculine hand stretched avengingly towards Mr Binnacle. For a tiny fraction of time it had him by the scruff of the neck. The next moment the avenger stared distractedly at the torn remnants of a well-laundered gladstone collar which was all his hand retained of Mr Binnacle ; and Mr Binnacle, with an exultant gasp, leaped into the narrowing aperture of the gates. But he was just one second too late. Like gigantic fingers, like the iron talons of fate, they seized the little man, nipped him smartly, and held him, all wriggling arms and legs, in their cruel grip. For one nauseating moment of writhing and screaming Mr Binnacle seemed to have as many limbs as a spider.

The crowd gulped its horror, and remained for a brief while in a coma of inactivity. Then mutterings, gasps, sighs, and panic cries rose and became blended in a symphony of terror, a muted music. You could almost hear the agitated drum-taps of a hundred human hearts ; yet the total effect was that of an ungainly monster, a hydra-headed thing, breathing impotent compassion. When, here and there, a woman fainted, it was as if one of the myriad muscles of the creature relaxed into immobility ; when men darted forward to the rescue (for the hesitancy was less than a second in duration), they appeared to be no more than the monster's exploring tentacles.

Some such image as this, even in the midst of that horror, presented itself to the mind of the pale young man in spectacles who had been moved to audible but not forcible protest by Mr Binnacle's unmannerly manœuvres. By profession a literary journalist, by natural endowment an intellectual, Guy Upcott never wearied of affirming, in print, his identity with the crowd, his sympathy with its tastes and aspirations. Eager to escape the stigma of highbrowism, he was loud in his denunciation of those who stand aloof from popular enthusiasms. From time to time he contributed to the weekly reviews upon which he lived witty little papers on 'The Hypocrisy of Hypercritics,' and cognate matters. Every week, instead of going to church, he visited a picture palace and enjoyed himself religiously ; and once, in a commendable endeavour to live up to the spirit of his essay, 'In Praise of Beer,' he had entered a tavern and sadly consumed half a pint of pale ale. He was interested enough in bad popular fiction to become quite heated in its defence, but not interested enough to read it, still less write it. 'Art divorced from life is the merest vanity' he was fond of saying, and he pronounced the platitude defiantly, with the air of a discoverer. In his breast pocket he carried a tiny copy of Horace, which he read furtively and in secret, as though it had been an indecent publication liable to confiscation by the police.

Never was a heart more indubitably in the right place than was Guy Upcott's. This being so, he shared to the full the painful sensation that shuddered through the crowd. And yet, being introspective and a maker of phrases, he was, in spite of himself and his opinions, the most detached of all the spectators. He alone savoured the curious drama of the catastrophe even in the very moment of recoiling from its agony. He alone saw it as a picture, a remote and bizarre work of art. In the vision of that writhing, black-coated human insect, held there as if in derision, and as if as a warning to its fellows, he alone detected a hint at once of symbolism and of cosmic parody.

Both vision and agony were in fact short-lived. Already, before Upcott could conquer the paralysis of his body, the lethal gates had been opened, and the remains of poor Mr Binnacle lowered to the ground.

' Stand back ! Give him air ! ' cried some one, and numerous feet shuffled in response. But indeed Mr Binnacle had all the air he could possibly need, and more than all. Even to the inexpert eyes of the little cordon that guarded him it was evident that no life remained, or could remain long, in that mutilated body. From the platform which Mr Binnacle had desired so ardently to approach floated the sound of clanging gates and normal human voices. The machinery of life had already resumed motion. Men rode on to their offices, women to their shopping. One by one the crowd round Mr Binnacle filtered through the gates and went their way, averting their eyes from the corpse as they passed it. 'Shocking thing, shocking!' murmured the woman Mr Binnacle had butted. 'Must have been mad, poor fellow! But we can't stay here all day.' That seemed the general sentiment.

Only the active few remained, sombrely alert, awaiting the police ambulance, together with a handful of the idly curious and one or two insatiable gluttons in sensation. Guy Upcott remained, too, though he falls into none of these classes. Guy Upcott remained, burning with the knowledge of what he had seen, and wondering how far it tallied with what these others had seen. There was a hectic flush on his cheeks; his eyes shone with an excitement that was more than half fear; he felt unnerved, limp. Should he speak out, or should he keep silent? Like most men of his mental calibre he was constantly a prey to indecision, because his active mind never ceased in its task of marshalling the pros and cons of problems that to unsophisticated intelligences seem simple. Whether to do this or that caused him agonies of doubt, so innumerable and far-reaching were the consequences of either. He stood now, nervously stroking his chin, his mind occupied with his immediate problem, but not to the exclusion of lesser and even trivial things. His thumb and forefinger caressed the firm contours of his jaw, communicating a sensation which his mind translated into the thought that it was high time he bought some new razor-blades. The reflection mingled with the puzzle without distracting him from it. Razor-blades. There was a shop in the Strand. But had *they* noticed anything? That ticket-collector fellow—had *he* seen it? No, he had had his back to the train, no doubt. And if he, Upcott, told them, they would think him demented, or drunk.

When the police ambulance people arrived, Upcott awoke out of a reverie that had been in danger of becoming a trance. The medical officer made a brief examination of the upper part of the body, and shook his head. ' Quite dead,' he said, without apparent emotion, and then added, with a surprising note of protest in his voice, ' It's absurd ! '

' What do you mean ? ' Upcott heard himself ask.

' I mean what I say. That an accident such as this should prove fatal is preposterous. There's no sense in it.'

Upcott warmed towards a doctor so human as to give way to unprofessional irritation. Yet he felt stupidly inclined to argue the matter. ' Isn't it possible that the shock . . .' he began diffidently. ' Weak heart, perhaps. But, of course, you know best.'

The medical man nodded, curtly but not unkindly, and turned again to his work.

' You see,' added Upcott, with mounting fever, ' it must have been a ghastly shock.' He marvelled at his own loquacity.

No one answered him.

' Because,' he added, making a last desperate assault upon the silence, ' both legs were cut off.'

The doctor looked up sharply. Every one else stared, first at Upcott, then at the subject of this inquest. The lower part of the body was hidden by a light mackintosh with which one of the bystanders had with instinctive decency covered the dead man before hurrying away. The doctor had already removed the covering from face and trunk ; and now, with a swift but undramatic gesture, he uncovered the rest.

' Gawd 'elp us ! ' said the ticket-collector.

The legs had been cut off cleanly just above the knees. A surgical amputation could not have been neater or have left less blood. Nevertheless it was a sufficiently horrid sight to induce a sickness in every lay spectator.

' You appear to be the only witness with

eyes in his head,' said the doctor to Upcott. The voice seemed to come from a great distance. 'But there's one very queer circumstance still. Perhaps you can help us there, too?'

'I'm afraid not,' said Upcott, moving away. 'I know nothing more.'

Here was his chance to tell all that he had seen. But he let it pass. No man, least of all a medico, would believe a word of it. He cursed himself for having become entangled in this conversation.

'Excuse me, sir.' The police sergeant's voice. But not, thank heaven, addressing him.

'Yes,' said the doctor.

'The legs are cut off, sir. We can all see that. But *where are the legs?*'

'Exactly,' said the doctor.

For of Mr Binnacle's legs, from the knees downward, there was no trace.

2

Mr Binnacle, curiously numbed and quite unaware of the pother he had created, jumped into the train and took his seat. He felt lighthearted and lightheaded: indeed, a general levity, both of body and of mind, was his dominant sensation as soon as he began to recover from the shock of his struggle against time and against that mob of stupid people who did not know time's value. Mr Binnacle experienced the relief of one who wakes after a long night of evil dreams ; those last few seconds, now he came to reflect on the matter, had possessed a distinctly nightmarish quality. He was heartily glad they were past, never to be repeated ; and that he was safely in the train speeding towards the Eldorado of his hopes, Lombard Street. With reasonable luck he would be there before the hour struck : whereby his colleagues would be deprived of a great occasion for facetiousness and his juniors of a unique opportunity for secret and malicious triumph. Never yet had Mr Binnacle been late, as the world counts lateness. Mr Binnacle considered himself late when he reached the office ten minutes, instead of his usual fifteen minutes, before the scheduled time of arrival.

Yet in spite of this deep-seated feeling of satisfaction Mr Binnacle was dimly aware of having lost something. What could it be ? Ah, his morning paper, of course ! And—infinitely worse—his umbrella ! 'Tut-tut-tut-tut !' said Mr Binnacle, employing his favourite oath. But even this disaster could not entirely quench his exhilaration.

Lost in his happy dreams of lifelong punctuality, Mr Binnacle did not at first notice the odd behaviour of the people who shared the compartment with him. A man of regular habits, he took most things for granted, expected folks to behave normally. There was a kind of unwritten compact between the world and Mr Binnacle. 'You play no tricks on me, and I play no tricks on you. We understand one another.' He had entered that railway compartment in the expectation of travelling four stages east accompanied by men and women as sober and almost as sensible as himself. But before he had been seated five minutes, panting after his unwonted exertions and gazing rather dizzily at the glossy toe-caps of his shoes, he became aware that something was wrong with the world. He glanced up to find himself half surrounded by a group of agitated human beings. They kept their distance, as though they were afraid of him ; and the distaste and fear that stared out of a dozen pairs of eyes gave colour to the conjecture that something alarming was happening. Mr Binnacle was baffled by the difficulty of reconciling two contrary impressions ; for it seemed to him that he both was and was not the object of interest. He was certainly the centre of the half circle formed by these agitated persons ; and, just as certainly, it was not upon him that their eyes focussed. In that first startled moment of apprehension it appeared to Mr Binnacle that the very toe-caps at which he had himself been staring were the object of this unmannerly and insane scrutiny. Whereupon he became exceedingly indignant. This was a display of cheap humour. This was parody. He had amused his fellow-passengers by gazing mutely, not unlike a baby, at his own toes ; and they, having no breeding, had conspired to make game of him.

There was only one way of treating that kind of insolence. It was altogether beneath notice. Mr Binnacle maintained an extremely dignified silence, and he sat as rigid as a statue. But not for long. As an assiduous correspondent to his local press, he could not resist exploring in his mind the rhetorical possibilities of the situation ; and when he had found certain salutary phrases it was inevitable that, sooner or later, they should demand utterance. Every artist will appreciate the nature of that inward need, that impulse to make literature. The literature that Mr Binnacle achieved on this occasion was not, perhaps, of the first quality.

' Gross insult to a respectable citizen ! ' he

flung out at his silent inquisitors ; and even to himself the remark sounded like a newspaper headline. 'I pity your ignorance of how gentlemen should behave,' he added ; and even Mr Binnacle realised, the moment after, that his wife's charwoman would have expressed her indignation in identical terms. His third and final thrust was more in character. 'If this is the New Humour,' said Mr Binnacle, 'I prefer the old.' And he emitted that queer little whistling melody, in two triumphant notes, with which the simple contrive to round off and emphasise their repartee.

The effect of these stern rebukes was disappointing. Nothing could have fallen flatter. No one took the least notice of them. No voice was raised in acknowledgment of Mr Binnacle's pity, or in defence of the New Humour. The statement that he was being grossly insulted was received in blank silence. Mr Binnacle now began to appreciate the sinister quality of that silence. It was abysmal, terrific; the silence of annihilation itself. In rising terror he looked from face to face of that staring crowd ; and, his senses becoming more acute, he saw, with a pang of sick fear, that their lips were moving, as in speech, and their hands and arms twitching in gesticulation. It penetrated his understanding that these people were talking among themselves, talking in some hideous soundless fashion of their own. Some invisible barrier cut him off from his fellows, a sound-proof but not a sight-proof curtain. It was not that he was stone deaf; nothing so simple. He could hear his own voice perfectly. The whole affair was incredibly complicated and terrifying. Another unpleasant fancy assailed him. It insinuated itself into his mind in the form of a question, Why did nobody look at him? Why had nobody, from the moment of his entry, spared him the merest glance? Was he invisible? And if so mad an idea could be entertained, by what mysterious compulsive force were these folks grouped around him, like iron filings attracted towards a magnet? If they were not concerned with him, with what *were* they concerned? To see and yet not be seen; to be articulate, even eloquent, yet not audible save to oneself; to be deaf to all sounds but the sound of one's own voice —the puzzle was too preposterous. Now Mr Binnacle knew well that everything outside the Bible is capable of rational, scientific explanation; and, as he retained a smattering of physics from his schooldays, he began trying to calculate the comparative velocity of heat, light, and sound. But even when he had the answers he did not know what to do with them.

All these thoughts and fears had occupied no more than a few seconds of time, and during those few seconds Mr Binnacle had remained rigidly still. But now, in sheer weariness, he relaxed a little. His movement, slight though it was, was evidently noticed by the watchers ; for those who were nearest stepped hurriedly back a pace, treading on the toes of those behind, though even now they did not raise their eyes to Mr Binnacle's bewildered countenance. Unused to being so pointedly ignored, the little banker had never felt so small in his life. For his comfort he conjured up a vision of the many office-boys who had quailed at his approach, the several young lady typists who held him in esteem. Suddenly Mr Binnacle gave a little bark of triumph and relief. The obvious explanation of it all flooded his being with new life. 'Of course,' said Mr Binnacle. 'This is something I've eaten. A mere dream.' Being nothing if not orthodox, he pinched himself by way of test. A good hard pinch, and it hurt not a little. 'Now was that a real pain, or a dream-pain ?' Truth to tell, the dream-hypothesis did not convince him. 'But that, too,' he argued, 'is quite consistent. My very lack of conviction is itself convincing, for if I knew I was dreaming I should wake up, and then I shouldn't be dreaming.' Into these pretty involutions we need not follow him. Mr Binnacle himself was not in the least deceived by them, ardently though he desired to be. His imagination had already secretly committed him to another and a far more dreadful belief.

And now, a new plan presenting itself, he stretched out his right hand to repeat his pinch, but this time it was to be bestowed on another man's arm. His fingers closed on nothingness. They gaped and groped in vain, like the mouthing of a goldfish. Was he then a disembodied spirit companioned by the dead? Intangible, inaudible, yet visible world—horror without end! He seized his own hands, one in the other; and each to the other seemed insubstantial as air, yet to itself, and in itself, solid and sensible. He sank back in his seat, exhausted by the maddening anxiety of it all. And he crossed his legs.

He crossed his legs, and it was as if he had drawn a six-chambered revolver and threatened the crowd with it. The watchers changed in a trice from a more or less orderly group of people, harassed by doubt and fear, to a mob that palpitated with panic, a mob possessed by one idea only, to escape from that compartment. Just at that moment the train drew into British Museum station, and the passengers poured out pell-mell. Mr Binnacle admired the British Museum only one degree less than he admired Madame Tussaud's Exhibition, but if this haste to alight from the train was born of enthusiasm for that invaluable institution, he thought the enthusiasm excessive. No, it would not do. These people were British business men, not foreign tourists ; and he himself, Percy Binnacle, was the cause of their panic haste. In some way altogether beyond his conjecture he was exceedingly distasteful to them. A baffling problem ; for, after all, his being a ghost, if ghost he were, signified nothing. Those others had been every whit as ghostly. Really, there was only one hypothesis that could explain all the facts ; yet in that hypothesis he could not bring himself to believe. If only he had been able to call it a dream and have done with it, he could have endured any further unpleasantness without wincing.

He was now alone in the carriage, in sole possession. Another man might have been flattered. Captain Hook, for example, would have relished the implied tribute. But Mr Binnacle did not like it at all. Mr Binnacle had his share of vanity, and even of snobbery ; but at heart he was a very sociable man, sociable in that he preferred to travel in the company of his fellows even though he never dreamed of indulging in idle conversation with them. He liked to know that they were there. And now he was dismally, dreadfully conscious that they were not there.

Only one human being was left in sight, the man in uniform, opener of doors and shouter of stations. He, when he had pulled the lever that caused his gates to shut with a ping, stood for one moment as if listening to the sibilant responses. The sound of the other closing gates, in a diminishing series, crashed like surf up the length of the platform. Then only, when the train had started moving, he turned to examine the interior of this apparently plague-stricken carriage. He put his face against the glass panel of the door and stared in.

Mr Binnacle saw him staring, saw the incredulous eyes, saw the mouth gaping in astonishment. The man's nose, flattened and broadened by being pressed against the window, made him resemble a bleached African negro. A shudder ran through Mr Binnacle. Better a whole trainload of invigilators than this grotesque and solitary persecutor! Mr Binnacle had the ghastly fancy that he was mad, and that this moving chamber was the very latest thing in padded cells. Or perhaps this train was all that was left of the world, a mechanical worm twisting and crawling for ever in a black infinity, himself the only passenger, and that flat-faced peering presence at the door the Almighty Conductor of an eternal, aimless tour. With such fantasies did Mr Binnacle beguile the journey between the British Museum and the Bank.

At the next station, when the conductor's scrutiny was withdrawn for a moment, Mr Binnacle sought cover. He got under the seat. And two stations beyond he rose to leave the train. But a new difficulty arose. The door of the carriage, which the man in uniform shewed no intention of opening, proved to be as intangible, as phantasmal, as the bodies of Mr Binnacle's former fellow-passengers. 'A certain proof that I am not dead,' argued the poor man, his teeth chattering with terror. 'For if I were a ghost I could float about freely enough.' Mr Binnacle had very precise ideas about the nature of ghosts, in whose existence he did not believe. Indeed there were moments in that strange incorporeal struggle for escape when he felt that he had in some measure surmounted the obstacle, moments when he felt himself to be half in and half out of the carriage. But while he stood agonising there, with the unseeing guard facing him behind a sheet of impalpable plate glass, the train started again. He was doomed to travel on to the terminus.

At Liverpool Street the guard flung open the carriage-door and peered in cautiously. His glance travelled quite beyond the object of its search. Then he stepped cautiously inside.

The next moment Mr Binnacle had darted out, and on to the platform, and was kicking and struggling blindly among phantoms. His feet experienced the joy of touching solid objects, but his fists beat nothing but air, and no squeals of pain reached his listening ears. How he escaped he never could have explained. He rushed to and fro, madly, like a demented dog, along the platform, up the stairs, strewing panic wherever he went. At last he emerged into the street.

'At all costs,' said Mr Binnacle, 'I must keep my head.' He might have added, 'what there is of it,' for his groping hands could find no evidence of his having a head at all.

'If only I keep cool, perfectly calm and collected, some reasonable explanation will present itself.'

Almost accustomed by now to exciting attention and alarm wherever he went, he was not surprised that half the people he met stared at his boots and then hastily crossed the road. He became aware, too, that a crowd had gathered and was straggling in his wake. It was evident that if he was the victim of a practical joke, all the world was involved in it. Perhaps he was merely drunk. Perhaps some one had drugged his wine. Perhaps this and perhaps that. He made a gallant effort not to go quite mad.

But fear got the better of him. Once again he broke into a sharp trot. The crowd pursued him. He could not hear their footsteps, but every time he glanced over his shoulder he saw their perspiring faces drawing nearer. He flung off his pursuers at length by dashing madly into the road, full though it was of swiftly moving traffic. The crowd was daunted.

With incredible agility he leaped, feet foremost, into an empty taxi that was roaming the streets in search of a fare. There for a while he was secure from observation. And when, twenty minutes later, he was disturbed by the entry of an old beau in a waisted frock overcoat, he had the luck to find another hiding-place in a public telephone-box labelled OUT OF ORDER.

There he remained for many hours, quivering with shame and fear and indignation. Then, in sheer weariness of spirit, he crept out again, and into the street. A newspaper placard was the first thing that caught his eye :

FATAL ACCIDENT AT A TUBE STATION

Mr Binnacle was beginning to learn the technique of his new life. He crept up behind the newsboy, who, providentially, happened to be engrossed in the examination of his own wares. Over the boy's shoulder Mr Binnacle read the report of his own accident. From the first word to the last amazing sentence he read it : ' The body has been identified as that of Mr Percy Binnacle, of Bolders Hill.'

Mr Binnacle stared, and stared again. Having had a surfeit of bewilderment, a very glut of terror, sheer annoyance was now his chief emotion. ' Whatever I am,' said Mr Binnacle firmly, ' I'm not dead. I'll sue this damned paper.'

He tried to tweak the ear of the phantom newsboy. 'Dead! Me dead!' he cried indignantly. He raised his arm to give himself that resounding slap on the chest which is the traditional symbol of robust life. But his hand fell on vacancy.

3

The epilogue is supplied by Jarve Bakeman, the nonagenarian sexton of the parish of Bolders Hill. For Bolders Hill, now a flourishing suburb containing five square miles of ready-made villas, was at one time a small village boasting nothing but a pump, a tavern, a grocery store, a parish church, and a post-office. Jarve Bakeman was the sole survivor from that time of Arcadian innocence, and with his round red wrinkled face, his bent back, his piping treble issuing from a toothless mouth, his soft eyes twinkling with innumerable memories, he looked the part. A solitary rustic in a region invaded by cockneys, he regarded the conquering race with kindly contempt. At certain times permitted by parliament he held court in The Green Man, throned in undisputed majesty in the inglenook of that ancient tavern. He allowed his inferiors to quench from time to time the royal thirst that burned within him, and, having drunk, he criticised their institutions with remarkable freedom. His satire of the new Bolders Hill, with its Dramatic Societies, its local parliament, its paved streets, its drainage system, and its fire brigade—all a pack of modern foolishness—kept his admiring audience in a perpetual titter. Not seldom he would discourse of his trade, which he still carried on with unabated vigour and relish. He had a taste for irony, had Jarve Bakeman, and death he was pleased to regard as the supreme irony. His remarks about the dear departed had been known to shock even the youngest of his listeners. The idea got about that Jarve himself, who in his person and speech so much resembled a sardonic deity, was himself immortal; that he had purchased immunity by a life of enthusiastic gravedigging.

There was, therefore, an unparalleled sensation in The Green Man when Jarve appeared one morning, palsied with fright. For a time no coherent speech could be coaxed from him. His friends plied him with medicine, however, and at length he told his story. I cannot pretend to do justice to Jarve's story; for it was decorated with blasphemies that would infallibly give offence to sober readers. But the substance of his narrative was that he had had a nightmare, the most grotesque and horrible of nightmares. His audience were vastly diverted, not believing a word he said. They had always known old Jarve to be a prime liar, but to-day, really he was surpassing himself. They slapped their thighs appreciatively, and bellowed with laughter. But the old man ignored these antics. He continued his tale.

In the middle of the night, he told them, he had been wakened, by nothing human, and kicked violently out of his bed. He could not see the face of his assailant ; he could see only his legs, cut short of the knees. He could see these legs, and he could feel them. They kicked him with extreme vigour. There seemed to be a certain purpose behind their mad activity. Poor old Jarve tottered from the room. The legs pursued him, drove him on. They drove him to the shed where his tools were kept. He snatched up a spade and gave fight, but the legs were too quick for him.

Great beads of perspiration formed on the old man's face as he described, with much vain repetition, that fight in the toolshed. It lasted ten minutes or more, but from the first he was hopelessly mastered. A hale old man, he was yet not as spry as he had been,

LAST DAYS OF BINNACLE 171

He remembered the time . . . (interlude for reminiscences of young manhood). Brought back to the story, Jarve told how at length he had taken to his heels again, driven by this pair of persecuting legs. They goaded him on, with many a brutal kick, until he reached the churchyard. There, as if by common consent, both pursuer and pursued came to a standstill. Jarve, by now thoroughly unmanned, waited humbly for instructions. He watched the legs prance in a devilish delirium of joy upon a newly made grave. Poor Mr Bickernel's grave it were, said Jarve, with an air of piety that sat oddly upon him. A flash of inspiration set him digging like a madman at poor Mr Bickernel's grave.

At this point Jarve Bakeman became thirsty, and for ten full minutes silently declined to do anything but sip, very negligently, the schooner of ale brought him by the excited barmaid.

'What then?' cried his tantalised cronies, gathering round him in a frenzy of impatience. 'Out with it, Jarve! Good old Jarve! Speak up, old dear! We've alwis bin good pals, aint we, Jarve!'

'When so be as I'm ready,' said Jarve, with great deliberation, 'I'll tell 'ee, my laddies.'

They waited his pleasure.

'Well, then,' said Jarve. 'When I'd dug me liddle ole, *in* me lord jumps. What else?'

There was silence for a space. 'And you buried 'im, like?'

Jarve winked over the edge of his pewter pot. 'Trust me,' said he grimly. 'And back to me bed I do go.'

Old Jarve was certainly in form to-day, said the listeners to each other, with many a delighted nudge.

THREE SUNDAYS

THREE SUNDAYS

SITTING in Kennedy's flat, our eyes glazed by the brightness of the gas-fire, we had been talking, we four journalists, of the sensation called time, a sensation wherein, as it has always seemed to me, one hovers upon the very verge of the ultimate reality. If we could understand ourselves, our incredible yet indubitable continuity, the first and last secret would have been told. The present, the little prison in which our consciousness is pent, is a unique combination that can never be repeated ; the past, once equally present, exists only in memory ; the future, only in expectation. Yet these three are so evidently mere arbitrary divisions in a single movement or flux that the mind cannot profitably consider them to be valid. Commonplaces such as these had passed between us, for in these small hours of the morning we were off-duty, as it were, and under no obligation to be clever in our conversation. I, for my part, was in that state of dazed wakefulness which long abstention from sleep, to say nothing of food, sometimes induces. The mood that dominated all four of us was lucid, serious, and confiding.

'Have you noticed,' said some one, 'how one's own past, however wretched, becomes mellow and beautiful in age, like wine ? There were things in my own childhood, for example, that cast a strong shadow over all my adolescence. Yet now, horrible as they were, I can think of them without pain. Indeed, to contemplate them gives me something of that curious impersonal pleasure which one gets from a piece of grim fiction. I could almost believe it *is* fiction, so remote is that poor little schoolboy from the fellow I now am.'

The speaker was a man of forty five, the oldest, by far, of our company. His name is immaterial to the story. After a short silence he spoke again : 'Does any one of you three happen to know why I changed my name ? '

We looked at each other with startled enquiry. Before anyone could answer, our friend added : 'The famous case of Mrs Merrill was before your time, of course.'

I laughed, to relieve the growing tension. 'My dear chap, if there's a story, let's have it.'

And so we had it.

THREE SUNDAYS

I

I see my childhood (said our storyteller) as a study in green gloom : it may be for the superficial reason that we had a green fence round our villa-garden, green venetian blinds in our windows, and a green, bleak chapel in which we spent the most significant hours of every Sunday ; or it may be, as I would rather suppose, because there is a quality in dark green, a cold austerity, an inimical strangeness, that seems characteristic of that time. I was a lonely little boy, having failed, as it seems to me now, to achieve real intimacy with any human soul. My mother died when I was eight, before I was mature enough to begin to understand what she meant to me. I remember, even now with some disgust, the mournful self-importance with which I reacted to that event. If the eye of a schoolmaster rested upon me in sympathy I preened myself with morbid pleasure. I would pause in my play and let sadness overwhelm me, and when the other children questioned my silences I would make a palpable excuse that deceived no one. I did not calculate these effects, but I took, subconsciously, a pleasure in them for a day or two. Animal spirits alone saved me from becoming a confirmed and detestable little prig. Riotous games, natural mischievousness, drove the worst kind of silliness out of me. But I remained introspective : I was lonely without being aware of my loneliness. My father, stricken by his bereavement, retired into himself like a wounded animal that crawls into its private lair to die. My efforts to get into touch with him availed nothing. I told him my secret thoughts, my solemnly conceived ambitions ; but in his profound lethargy he could not even pretend to an interest in these toys of the mind. He could give me nothing but an habitual, absent-minded affection.

At home we had a succession of queer, unsatisfactory housekeepers. They seemed to pounce upon us from the advertisement columns of a church newspaper, worry us for a while with their sulks or their loquacity, their bad cooking or their bad tempers, and then fly away, as upon a broomstick, in quest of new victims. There were long intervals when we were without any domestic help at all, and then my father would entirely neglect his meagre little business in the city and devote himself angrily to dusting and scrubbing and preparing meals of which I was the heartier participant. Such periods, though I naturally came in for my share of the drudgery, were on the whole pleasanter to me than the presence of a strange, uncongenial woman. They brought us, father and son, into a closer and kindlier relationship ; and they gave to us both a vision of the impossible, perfect housekeeper who would some day descend out of heaven to lift these burdens from our shoulders. Yet it was this vision, which became our chief support, that proved my poor father's undoing.

Setting aside the hours spent at my day-school, which constituted for me a brighter and more vital world, it was, I think, my Sundays that I most enjoyed. For unquestionably I extracted a certain enjoyment from the idle ruminations that filled my mind throughout that dedicated day. I liked chapel-going : not positively, but for the sake of the relief it afforded from my home-atmosphere. It released my hands from domestic duties and my mind from scholastic cares. The thought of home lessons, that bugbear of the day-boy, did not attend me in the house of God. I was free to indulge any and every fancy that visited me. We were more fortunate, too, than some others of our persuasion in that we had an actor in the pulpit. The Reverend Anthony Pruce, long-faced, lantern-jawed, with wild hair and bulging eyes, could generally be relied upon to supply first-rate sensation. 'The wicked are like chaff,' he would say, with sinister rapture ; and his cupped hands would stretch over the pulpit's edge holding imaginary chaff, and from his own large mouth would proceed the wind that scatters the wicked. His finest performances he reserved, with a nice discrimination, for the evening services, when the atmosphere would be more congenial to his master-purpose, that of making one's flesh creep. In a church dim with a palpable green gloom, which the tiny gas-jets served only to make visible, he would treat us to selections from his repertoire, which was, indeed, no bad one. It was from the Reverend Anthony, at all events, that I got my first taste of Shakespeare.

Sunday, then, was not unwelcome to me, and it is with Sunday, by an odd chance, that the three crises of my childhood are associated. Looking back, one sees the whole disaster as an inevitable movement, a dramatic curve, which first became visible on the occasion of Miss Ebner's Sunday visit. Miss Ebner, whose advertisement had attracted my father, came to be interviewed on a certain Saturday afternoon in November, within a week of my twelfth birthday. She was approved, and my father offered to engage her on the spot. No sooner was the offer made, however, than she began to exhibit a curious reluctance to accept the very position she had been eager to apply for. This hesitation set the seal on my father's decision, and, anxious not to lose her, he urged Miss Ebner to come the next day and take social tea with us, so that the matter could be further discussed. I myself knew nothing of this until my return, covered in mud from the football field, just as dusk was falling. And so, on Sunday afternoon, she presented herself : a tall, gaunt, sallow-faced woman of fifty or more. Was this the perfection my father had led me to expect ? She was a meagre woman in everything but height. Her skin had a leathern look, highly polished. Black eyebrows met across the top of her nose ; black, sticky hair was coiled in ropes upon her head. I disliked her at sight, profoundly and irrationally. My dislike was intemperate. Most of all I hated her hands, which, in offensive contrast to the rest of her, were plump and pink and provided with a bunch of fat fingers that looked like little beef-sausages. I hated to meet the glances of her glittering, bead-like eyes ; I shivered at the sound of her affected, drawling speech. And, finally, I resented her attitude to myself.

'Is this your little boy ? ' she cried to my father, in a rapture. 'Why, he's quite a man, isn't he! Will he make friends with me?'

The hatred I conceived for her in that moment may have coloured my judgment of her person. I suspected her of deliberate satire, wherein I was probably unjust. Dense though she appeared in general, she was quick enough to sense my dislike, and from time to time made elaborate and clumsy attempts to win favour with me. My father she had already conquered, and for that alone I could never forgive her. It was evident that he was bent on engaging her. He watched her every movement with an eagerness that the occasion rendered grotesque. After an hour's insipid talk, she rose to go.

'Good-bye, sonny,' she said to me, with a brilliant smile. She fumbled with my hand for a moment, and when I withdrew it I had a half-crown sticking to my palm. That was a bad moment for me. I knew the value of a half-crown as well as any other schoolboy, but I could accept nothing from this enemy.

'Thank you, Miss Ebner,' I said, in my politest manner. 'But I'd rather not have it.'

'Yes, yes,' she said. 'Take it, sonny, and buy yourself some candy or . . . a nice top.'

I stared at her coldly. 'I shall put it in the missionary box,' I remarked.

THREE SUNDAYS

Before she could reply I was at the sideboard, making good my words. I released that fabulous coin into the slit; the sound of its fall cut short her protest. She shrugged her shoulders, smiled wanly, and followed my father into the hall.

He came back after seeing her to the door.

'Well, Geoff! How do you like Miss Ebner?'

'I can't bear her,' I said.

'Nonsense!' cried my father. 'You like her very much, my boy. Do you hear?'

He pointed his little brown beard at me, and his blue eyes flashed anger.

'Do I really?' I retorted, with precocious insolence. 'My mistake, father. I thought I hated the woman.'

We scowled at each other for a few seconds. Then he turned on his heel, and left me to my miserable thoughts.

2

My second eventful Sunday came several months later. I returned from an unseasonable visit to a rural aunt's, to find Miss Ebner permanently installed in my father's house. Aunt Sarah had dropped enough dark hints to put a duller boy than I in full possession of the facts. But I would not bow to the inevitable : I faced it with implacable hostility. We met, she and I, at the breakfast table on Sunday morning, she having been confined to her bedroom with a headache on the night of my homecoming. My father hovered about us, an uneasy master of ceremonies. I pitied him, little beast though I was ; but I would not spare him.

The woman rose to greet me.

'Good morning,' I said.

My father's eyes flashed daggers at me. 'Now then, Geoff my boy !' he said sharply. 'Kiss your new mother !'

'Mother's dead,' I muttered.

I did not know how cruel I was being ; but, had I known, I could have done no other. The idea of kissing this creature revolted every nerve in my body and every sentiment in my heart. I felt that I was being asked to endorse a monstrous and insane infidelity. My father, I fancy, was on the point of tears ; and, to save himself from breaking down, he raised his voice to a shout.

'Do as you're told, sir !'

There being no help for it, I pecked shamefacedly at the cheek held out for my salute.

'Good morning, mater,' prompted my father.

'Good morning, Mrs Merrill,' I said.

3

From that to the end was a period of not quite two years, during which my father came more and more to my way of thinking. What mad fancy propelled him towards her in the first place I have yet to learn. He himself was not at an ardent age, and she was his senior by several years. She possessed no personal attractiveness. Was it possible that her parody of a Gioconda smile had fascinated him? In my eyes that smile became more sinister every day, and there is no question that it became more satirical. She conceived a violent, mysterious grudge against my father within a few weeks of marriage. It was heralded by a tragic mood, which set her pacing up and down the kitchen like a caged vixen, wringing her hands and muttering, 'The past! I want the past!' My father remonstrated with her, not in the blustering fashion he used towards me, but with a patience, an air of pleading, that was painful to witness. 'My dear, not in front of the boy! Try to control yourself.' At that she looked at him with a cruel, half-crazy smile, and held out her fat hands. 'Give me the past, Richard! Give me back the past.'

I think she was perhaps a little mad that day. At tea-time she suddenly broke out, in the middle of an ordinary conversation, 'Ah, Richard, you ought not to have done it.'

'Done what, my dear?'

'You ought not to have married me for my money.'

The poor man was in despair. 'You know that's not true, Mildred. You say such things only to hurt me.'

She stared at him for two minutes without speaking, with a curl in her lip that made the scrutiny an insult. Her fingers were busy the while rolling tiny pellets of bread, a pile of which she already had beside her plate.

'Well?' she said at length, just as though he had not answered her. 'Well, Richard?'

'I don't understand you,' said my father.

'Tell me,' she urged, poking her face confidentially towards him. 'Now that you've got us, me and my money, what are you going to do with us?'

With a desperate effort to save the situation my father turned to me and resumed our interrupted conversation. 'Mr Mansell thinks you'd stand quite a chance, Geoff, in the College of Preceptors examinations. Would you like to try?'

My stepmother cut in with a little scornful laugh. 'No, Richard. Don't waste my money like that. He'll never pass.'

'Why shan't I pass?' I demanded truculently.

'Poor Geoffrey!' she sighed, shaking her head at me. 'He's not a sharp boy.'

My father was something of a sermon-taster; and, being unable to share my delight in the Reverend Anthony's performances, he sometimes led expeditions to remoter Bethels. There was one in particular, a poky little place situated in a mean street three miles away. The suburb to whose spiritual life it ministered was even more drab and dejected than our own. The very idea of the place remains a plague-spot on my imagination. To reach it one had to pass through a slum-area full of dull-eyed, sour-smelling children who watched one's every movement with furtive curiosity. I recall a trifling incident that summed up for me, in one vivid symbol, the blight that had fallen upon that poverty-stricken region. A slatternly woman stood at her door fiercely awaiting the return of her errant son. He, a miserable little four-year-old, eyed her fearfully from the road. 'Come along, Georgie! I ain't going to 'it cher, dearie.' Fortified by the assurance, he approached her slowly. She held out her arms to him in coaxing appeal ... and the next moment her left hand had caught him by the scruff and her skinny fist was cuffing him with fury. A piteous blubbering filled the evil street ; the door slammed, cutting short the sound ; and in the cold dead silence that followed I clutched my father's arm, feeling him to be my one refuge in a universe devastated of faith. Beyond the scene of this outrage lay the cemetery in which my mother was buried, a nightmare region advertised in all the little streets that environed it. All the paraphernalia of death were visible in the shop-windows ; hanging signs announced ' Funerals furnished ' and ' Wreaths in half an hour ' ; a mason's yard assaulted my imagination with memorial crosses and truncated columns and chubby Victorian angels wrought in stone. The sight of these things in the grey dusk of a winter's evening made me miserable for days, but I concealed my mortuary thoughts ; and my father, with other troubles of his own, and intent, moreover, on some theological tit-bit that only his special preacher could supply, never guessed that this reiterated experience scored an indelible mark on my mind. Between husband and wife there was now no open warfare ; they lived together, as it seemed to me, in a misery mitigated by long periods of comparative cheerfulness. But her secret grudge remained, and the knowledge of it told upon him. I, for the most part, was kept in the dark about their relationship, after that first outburst which I have described. It was not until nearly two years had passed that, returning with them both from one of these dismal Sunday excursions, I caught my second glimpse of her unsleeping malice.

The night was dark and cold. My iron-tipped schoolboy boots clattered on the pavement, a reassuring sound. I had hold of my father's left arm, and he, with his right, guided the smooth, noiseless footsteps of his wife. Silence had fallen upon us. The subject of our preacher's daring heresies, so dear to my father, had been exhausted. Quite suddenly, out of the darkness, came the woman's plaintive voice, edged with conscious cruelty: 'Oh, Richard, give me back the past. Why didn't I marry a man of some education, a gentleman!' I could have burst into tears when my father replied, like a hurt child: 'Am I not a gentleman, Mildred?' She sniggered, and said nothing. It was as though the question were too ridiculous to need reply. No other word was spoken during that walk. We took our supper in silence. After the meal my father sat down at our little, yellow-keyed piano, and tinkled out a few melodies from 'The Messiah.' The music, intimately associated with my mother, stirred poignant memories in us both. I listened with aching heart, wondering how he could bear so to torment himself. I wanted to draw close to him; I yearned to make him understand that he was not unloved. But the profound emotions of boyhood are inarticulate; and I let my one chance pass. I sat, mute and still, in the stuffy little, dim-lit parlour that contained all I loved and all I hated. We watched him, the woman and I : she with cold smiling malignity, I with I know not what misery in my eyes. He broke off suddenly in his playing, seemed to search his memory for a moment, and, then after a wistful glance at me, he again began fumbling over the keys made sacred by the touch of other and more skilful fingers. At first I could not seize the significance of the tune he was struggling to render; then, with a swift uprush of the past, I heard my mother's voice :

Peace be with all souls de-part-ed

The burden, whether my father's or my own, became intolerable. Incontinently I fled the room, and went to bed.

4

It must have been two hours later that I awoke from unhappy dreams with the sound of a nightmare cry ringing in my ears. It quavered off into a series of terrible coughs, succeeded by a shrill whistling endlessly protracted. I sprang from my bed, every nerve twitching. Silence supervened. Had I indeed been dreaming? As I stood there, in an agony of doubt and fear, the door of my room began moving towards me, and a face, the face of my stepmother, was thrust into the aperture.

'Geoffrey dear,' she cried softly.

'Come in. Come in. What's the matter? I heard an awful row.'

She entered, dressed in her night-clothes, stringy black hair hanging in rats' tails about her shoulders. She carried a candle, whose light made visible the quivering excitement in her face. She appeared to be intoxicated with fear.

Impatient of her smiling, staring silence, I seized her by the arm and repeated my question urgently. 'Is father all right?'

'Geoffrey,' she said, in a husky whisper, 'you must run and get help, there's a good boy. Your poor father's out of his mind.'

'Out of his . . . !' I could not repeat the terrible phrase.

'Mad, my boy, mad.' Her eyes glistened at me. 'Run and rouse the neighbours. I'm afraid to be left with him.'

I strode to the door. 'I'm going to see my father first,' I said hotly. For even in this moment of crisis I could not but detest the woman.

She ran and clung to my arm. 'Very well, dear. We'll go together.'

We tiptoed, like conspirators, down the corridor that divided my room from theirs. At the door she seemed to hesitate; but I pushed her roughly aside, and stepped in.

My father lay, singularly at peace, in a bed of blood. From his throat projected the handle of a kitchen-knife.

I felt my senses slipping away. Darkness rushed into my eyes. And then, with an abrupt recovery, I think I shouted; for the next moment my stepmother was at my elbow and peering up at me.

'Hush!' she said, finger on lip, eyes wide with portent. 'We must humour him, child. He's quite mad. I *told* him his face was going green,' she added, with a giggle, 'and he denied it, poor fellow!'

THE SUNFLOWERS

THE SUNFLOWERS

DUSK was falling. In a moment or two Aunt Hester would call, standing, a black figure of doom, in the kitchen doorway. Bedtime yawned like the jaws of a dragon eager to appease its appetite on a diet of little girls. Once in bed, with the light out, you are in an enchanted country, it is true. You have only to keep your eyes tight shut to see pink mountains and purple skies and golden rain falling, a world wrought in bright dust, a heaving sea of many colours. But enchantment is dangerous as well as exciting. Those black ravines and the green catseyes that puncture their blackness, those are less welcome. And sometimes you feel yourself falling, falling, into a dark void and out again, with all space, all the queer dim colours of nothingness, spinning round you. It is like the switchback at the Crystal Palace, only much worse or much better, as your luck determines. And soon your fancies, if you fail to keep a firm grip on them, will get quite out of control. They will stamp and chafe and toss their manes, like a herd of zebras, and whirl you away to the bottom of the deep pit of sleep. At the bottom of the deep pit you must lie, then, at the mercy of whatever dreams choose to visit you. Angels of God, if Aunt Hester is to be believed, have been deputed to keep watch and ward, angels specially trained for the protection of children from all night-fears; but, with so many bad bogies getting through the celestial cordon, one is forced to suppose that angels are not what they were in Aunt Hester's time: they, too, it would seem, have their sleepy moments, and discipline among them has been relaxed. Some of Sheila's dreams were so bad that she could not even speak of them, months afterwards, without tears welling up in her big dark eyes. Once she had dreamed that she saw two leering gentlemen, dressed like cricket umpires, emerge from her parents' bedroom carrying between them a bowl full of blood; she knew, in her dream, that these creatures had killed Father and Mother and now reigned in their stead, and she shuddered to see the hideous irony in their eyes as, with infinite care, they closed the bedroom door. A very long time ago that must have been; for Mother was but a memory now, a rather dim memory, dimmer by far than the terror of the dream itself.

So Sheila had better reason than most to fear bedtime. And to-night she had an additional reason. Three weeks or more ago her father had gone away (in search of Mother, perhaps), and now Sheila's ageing sorrow had been illuminated by an idea, an inspiration. She stood in the kitchen garden and gazed with ritual devotion upon the three feet of earth where her name was growing in letters of mustard and cress. This was now her sanctuary ; this was one of the last works of her father's hand before that mysterious illness at the end of which, without saying good-bye, he had gone away. And she guessed that there was but little time left in which to effect her secret purpose.

Putting her hands together, she closed her eyes and whispered her prayer : 'Dear God, will you please ask my father to come back, because Helena is very lonely and so am I.' She waited confidently for God to answer her. He had spoken to people in the Bible ; why shouldn't He speak to her ? Struck by a sudden doubt, she went down on her knees and repeated her petition. Prayer uttered in an improper posture might never reach the divine ear at all, and, even if it did, might receive no attention. She waited for her answer. But the dusk gathered and no voice sounded, no vision appeared. The tall sunflowers, pursing up their faces for sleep, nodded near her, each peeping at her inquisitively (but not unkindly) with his single large brown eye. Intruders in the kitchen garden, great indolent creatures flaunting their flame in a region dedicated to utility, they yet seemed regally unaware of their intrusion. Uncle Peter had a fancy, which Sheila was glad to share, that a company of kings had missed their way home after an evening of revelry and had taken root, when the magic hour struck, by some sinister enchantment. To-night they seemed more than ever human, almost sympathetic, with no loss of their kingliness. Perhaps they, too, were eager for news of the vanished one.

No sign came from Heaven. But there was yet hope. God might be busy listening to some one else's prayers. He had so many people to attend to. But Jesus, who was specially the friend of little children, would surely answer her. To Jesus she therefore presented her new plea : 'Please ask God to let my father come back again. My father's name is Mr Dyrle.'

The silence remained, broken only by the

minute sounds of eventide. Slowly, as Sheila waited, the petals of the sunflowers drooped closer together, like strange yellow eyelashes veiling velvet eyes. In those few moments the first two Persons of the Trinity were weighed in the balance and found wanting. Sheila determined that if the Holy Ghost proved more responsive she would never bother with the others again.

'Sheila!'

A voice indeed, but not a voice from heaven. It was Aunt Hester calling her in to bed. Sheila lingered a while to give the Holy Ghost His chance.

'Coming, Auntie,' she called. 'O Holy Ghost, do be quick and answer!'

'Sheila!'—more insistently from Aunt Hester.

Sheila turned towards the house, her lip trembling. Her cup of bitterness was full. With a sudden impulse of fear she ran down the gravel path to meet Aunt Hester. She hid her face in Aunt Hester's skirt, weeping.

'My dear child!' cried Aunt Hester, 'what's the matter?'

The little girl spoke between sobs. 'They're all too busy to listen, Auntie. I don't like Them a bit, do you?'

2

Next morning Sheila had forgotten her troubles. She had lain all night at the bottom of the dark pit, shut away from the external world, inside herself, secure from interruption. In waking life nothing entered the wonderland of her imagination but suffered transmutation into something rich and strange. In sleep, perhaps, the contents of her mind, her accumulated memories and imaginings, broke loose from control and paraded before her in a grotesque cavalcade. Of late heaven had interested her perhaps unduly, but only because her father had recently become a resident there. Normally, she was not a theological child. There was a time when she had supposed heaven to be only a greater and more glorious Crystal Palace (for with God all things are possible). Now, when she thought of it, it appeared to be a place very much like Penlington Gardens, with a large railway junction attached, a region where all lost friends, even dolls, would be found again. She cherished the hope of finding even the Joneses there, notwithstanding their dinginess and their hatred of washing.

The Joneses had been Sydenham neighbours, but Sydenham, whence, with sister

Helena and the invalid father, she had been transported by her father's cousin Hester (Sheila's aunt by courtesy), was already a fast-fading picture in her mind. From Hugo and Monica Jones she had caught a passion for keeping tadpoles in a jam-jar, and silk-worms in a cardboard boot-box ; but here, in the house at Penlington, such habits were discouraged. But Hugo and Monica were trifling losses to set against the great gains of Penlington. True, there was no front garden now, but there were iron railings, an iron gate, a series of broad stone steps leading to the front door, and a big hall ; and, at the back, a small square garden enclosed by a wall. At the back, half a mile distant, was a junction of many railway lines. Sheila and the trains were great friends. The sound of them was seldom out of her ears. Sometimes at night she lay in bed listening to their gruff voices ; sometimes she crept to the window to watch their lithe dark bodies, which sparkled with points of light. She wondered often whence they came and to what dark land they travelled. She tried to imagine who the people could be that went on these mysterious journeys. One traveller, she pretended, was a thin grey-bearded man who carried with him a glossy black bag like Father's ; but what that bag contained she could never quite decide.

Of comparatively pleasant things, such as these, Sheila may have dreamed during the night that followed her ineffectual prayer in triplicate. For in her experience it was the horridest dreams that could be remembered most clearly ; and on this particular morning she remembered none at all. She had also forgotten even her disappointment with the Holy Trinity, and consented to say her prayers as usual, convinced that she would not live through the day if she omitted them. There were still interesting things left in her world after all. She pretended this morning to be discovering it all for the first time. There was that winding stairway with its half-way landing from which through a window she could see fields like golden seas ablaze with buttercups. Not far from that window there was a tall yellow-faced clock with a very musical voice. He smiled at her when she passed him. Following the stairway, she came to the place where the banister rail curled round upon itself ; and so to the red-tiled hall. From the hall there was a choice of four ways : a small door admitting to the garden ; the drawing-room, a sombre place containing a walnut piano and filled with a strange Sabbath smell ; a long passage leading to the double bliss of the kitchen and the coal-house ; and, lastly, the dining-room.

In the dining-room there was a wonderland known as Under-the-table, consisting mainly of four fat mahogany table-legs and a thick carpet with a pattern of blue, black, red and yellow. She had great adventures on this carpet, tracing out expeditions with her thumb and pretending that the black was coal, the red fire, and the yellow buttercup-fields or golden syrup, by turns. In the contemplation of these delights she lost account of Heaven's curious unresponsiveness to the petitions of little girls. In the dining-room, too, were chairs with twisted legs and with brown pads tied at four corners to their hard seats ; and there was a black cupboard, upon which, high and lifted up, dwelt a biscuit-tin decorated by the figure of a Chinaman.

While, after breakfast, she was rediscovering these things, Uncle Peter rediscovered her. Uncle Peter, whom she had known only three weeks, was fond of describing himself as a sour old bachelor of thirty three. Since his return from abroad some few months ago he had been her greatest friend. He was very different from his cousin, Aunt Hester, though she, too, was rather nice. Uncle

Peter was tall and had a red face; his wiry hair and bristly moustache were flame-coloured; and there were little wrinkles round his often twinkling eyes. A heavy gold chain stretched across his ample waistcoat. His voice, and that only, was faintly suggestive of the vanished Father.

'Hullo, She,' said Uncle Peter. 'What shall we do to-day?'

'Let's go to the gardens, Peter.'

So to Penlington Gardens they went, that paradise of velvet lawns, of fountains, of weeping willows whose branches reached the ground and made little shut houses filled with green light, of drowsily humming insects, of bright tropical-seeming flowers, of orange trees growing in scented hot-houses, of little lakes and reeds and grassy banks. On the largest of the lakes lived real swans who would eat bread, and there was a big enclosure in which dwelt rabbits, with tiny white tufts of tails, in all their native wildness.

At noon Uncle Peter—that marvellous man —produced a packet of sandwiches. Sheila danced round him in rapture.

'Now we shan't have to go back to lunch, shall we?'

'No fear,' said Uncle Peter.

'While we have our sandwiches,' said

Sheila, 'will you tell me a story? . . . I'm not too big to be told stories, am I?'

Uncle Peter looked judicial, pursing up his lips and cocking his head on one side.

'H'm! Five, isn't it?'

'Five and a half nearly,' Sheila corrected him.

Uncle Peter looked grave. 'Five and a *half*! Dear me!'

Anxiously, round-eyed, she waited for his verdict. 'Do you think it's too old?'

'Well,' said Uncle Peter. 'It *is* a great age, isn't it? We must be careful, you know.'

'Yes,' agreed Sheila.

'But, then,' cunningly added Uncle Peter, brightening a little, 'we could keep the story-telling a secret, couldn't we?'

'Oh, do you really think we could?'

Mystery and guilt gleamed in Uncle Peter's eye. 'Do you know, She, I believe I'll tell you a secret. Shall I?'

'Please,' she implored.

'Well, *I'm* thirty three, and I'm often told stories.'

She stared in wonder. 'What—just like a little boy?'

'Yes, you won't tell, will you?'

'Of course not. . . . Will you tell me the

story about the boy who had a penknife, please, Peter?'

There were at least three kinds of stories. There were the quite true Sunday stories like Joseph and the Coat of Many Colours—favourites these, of Aunt Hester's; there were fairy-tales which were very nearly true; and there were doubtful ones with morals. The Boy and the Penknife was Uncle Peter's own, and unique in being the only perfectly true story outside the Bible. It was about a boy whose mother gave him three pennies.

'What did she do that for?' asked Sheila.

'Because he never interrupted her stories, I fancy,' said Uncle Peter rather woefully. 'Well, as soon as he had got his pennies he ran off . . .'

'Didn't he——' began Sheila.

'. . . after thanking his mother, of course,' said Uncle Peter hastily. 'Ran off to look in a shop-window where there was a fine pen-knife he wanted.'

'A pearl one,' Sheila murmured.

'So he went in and bought it.'

'Yes, but first——'

'Oh, first he put his nose against the window-pane and gazed . . .'

'Until his nose got quite cold,' supplemented Sheila. 'It did last time, you know.'

'Quite right. Then, when he had bought it, he went to the river-side to cut bulrushes. All of a sudden . . .'

At this point in the narration Sheila began to feel very uneasy. There was, she knew, tragedy coming; a queer feeling was in her throat; - but she was determined not to spoil the story by remembering what came next.

'Did he fall in?' she asked.

'No,' said Uncle Peter. 'He nearly fell in, but not quite. But all of a sudden'—the listener held her breath—'his hand slipped and the knife sank to the bottom of the river.'

Sheila sat in wistful silence, her large eyes imploring the story-teller not to pause too long there. Her lip quivered in a way that made Uncle Peter hastily continue.

'But he didn't cry, this boy. Not he! And in time he grew to be a man.'

'Is it anyone I know?' asked Sheila, all innocence.

Gravely he nodded.

'The postman?'

'No.'

'The hairy man next door?'

'You mean our handsome neighbour with the brown beard, no doubt. No, it isn't him.'

'Who is it, Uncle Peter?'

'I am the man,' said Uncle Peter.

'*You!*' cried Sheila in astonishment. The same revelation had astonished her only a few days before.

'The very identical,' said Uncle Peter.

'What's that?'

'Have another sandwich,' replied Uncle Peter.

3

At tea-time, back in the house at Penlington, she confided to Aunt Hester in an unguarded moment of enthusiasm that they had seen a fairy.

'He was bathing in a buttercup,' added Sheila.

Aunt Hester held up an admonitory forefinger. 'Little girls mustn't tell stories.'

'My dear Hester!' cried Uncle Peter. His voice was infinitely weary, and its weariness seemed to lash poor Hester cruelly. She met his glance in dumb distress, as though he had whipped her, and then she turned her head away to look fixedly out of the window. Her lip trembled.

Aunt Hester was like that. A word from Uncle Peter would always subdue her. Sheila, staring with all her eyes, was frightened by the expectation of seeing Aunt Hester burst into tears. But the disaster was averted.

'Get on with your tea, darling,' said Aunt Hester gently, and the little girl, bending again over her plate, pondered the mystery of these two familiar yet remote creatures, between whom there existed a something that altogether transcended her understanding. By what virtue did Peter, that harmless and so friendly old gentleman of thirty three, exercise careless dominion over his prim cousin Hester ? Sheila recalled, as she bit a half-moon out of her slice of bread-and-butter, how it was at Peter's wish that the sunflowers had been suffered to remain in the kitchen-garden usurping space that belonged by right to more useful vegetation. Aunt Hester had said they must be dug up and transplanted. 'Oh, let them stay, my dear,' Uncle Peter had exclaimed. 'They're so delightfully discordant.' And Aunt Hester had blushed prettily : Sheila couldn't guess why.

Sheila was in a hurry to get down from table. But she dared not ask permission, because to-day there was an alien presence among them. Upstairs there lived an inconceivably ancient woman known as Granny. She lived in a huge chair, her feet on a hassock, at her side a spittoon, within her reach a bell-rope. She wore a black pleated bodice and a white cap. Her white and withered frailty was terrifying, so easily might her large face fall to pieces like an incandescent gas-mantle. She sat all day sipping peppermint, smelling salts from a bottle, making little grunting noises, opening and shutting (with a strange popping sound) her spectacle-case. And for hours she would hold close to her dim eyes her Book of Common Prayer and make pretence of reading the collect for the day. Seldom, indeed, did she descend from the Olympus to which her inhuman agedness entitled her, but whenever she did so it was to Sheila as if some colossal and indifferent deity had come amongst them. Most often these descents were made on behalf of visitors. Granny would make the perilous journey, assisted by her two grandchildren, in order to prove herself still queen of the household.

Inscrutable caprice had brought Granny to the tea-table to-day, and Sheila therefore itched for freedom. When at last she did escape she ran off to Camelot, the beautiful brick-field that backed on to the garden. This was forbidden ground, for Sheila was permitted to visit Camelot only in the company of the Madders girls, the eldest of which had given the place its name. But for the moment she forgot the prohibition. At first she thought

THE SUNFLOWERS

she would take Lady Betty with her for a treat, but a moment later that plan was abandoned. Lady Betty had recently been guilty of several acts of disobedience. She had resolutely refused to be fed ; she had knocked her medicine out of Sheila's hand ; and she had coughed shamelessly without attempting to turn her head away first. These things could not pass unpunished. Without proper discipline Sheila's large family of dolls—for were there not also Millicent and Agnes and Sammy the little black boy?—could never be brought up successfully. So Lady Betty, despite her tears ('And that's more than half temper too!' said Sheila), was left behind without ruth.

Camelot was an agreeable refuge. Sheila lay among the tall grasses and watched the insects running busily about their little world : ants going a-marketing, spiders that seemed to fly over the ground, so quickly did they move, and a red soldier who sometimes climbed up grass-blades and sat on the top of what must have been to him tall trees. Sheila followed the adventures of this brave soldier for a long while, saw with sympathy how he met and surmounted all the obstacles in his path. She wondered whether it was his mother who had made him his red coat, and whether she was very angry with him when he returned home from his rambles with torn clothes. After a while he disappeared under the grass and she saw him no more. A big dock-flower near by was nodding its head toward her, whispering something, she knew, but what she could not quite decide. She rather thought it was telling her a fairy-tale : of how in that little world of grass there dwelt a king who had a crown made of moss, and robes of thistledown, and who held his court under a toadstool. He had three sons, this king, and one day he said to them : 'Whichever of you kills the ladytoad that sits day and night upon this stool, for him I will build the finest palace in the world. It shall be made of chocolate cream, and there will be cherries growing in the garden all the year round. And whoever lives in it needn't ever go to bed till nine o'clock.' So the eldest son said : 'I'm the fellow for that job, being the eldest of your sons. The second is too fat, and the youngest only a baby.' But when he climbed, sword in hand, upon the neighbouring daisy and saw the big ugly toad squatting on that toadstool glaring about her, he was frightened and ran away. Then the second son said to his father, the king : 'I knew all along he would muff it. You watch me.' And off he went to the twine-shop kept by a grasshopper to buy some twine to tie the toad up with. While he was making these preparations, the third son, who wasn't a baby at all, climbed on to the toad-stool. 'Good morning!' said he to the lady-toad, 'how are you?' 'Nicely,' replied the toad, 'hoping you are the same as it leaves me at present. You're the king's son, aren't you?' 'Yes,' said the king's son, 'and I've come to kill you.' 'Thank you very much,' croaked the old toad. 'Kill away!' But when the king's son whipped out his sword and stuck it into the toad, she changed into a beautiful princess. And the young prince married her and they lived happily ever after in the finest palace in the world which the king with his own hands had built for them.

This was the tale the dock-flower told, as it nodded its head to Sheila and rocked to and fro.

'But that's one of Peter's tales,' said Sheila to the dock-flower. 'You know very well it is.'

The dock-flower, convicted of piracy, very wisely abstained from reply. But Sheila noticed that it had an ashamed look, very much the kind of look that Lady Betty always had when caught in the act of putting her fingers in the tea-cup.

Sheila was distracted by a little wailing cry. Something soft rubbed against her cheek, a fluffy ball of life, a stray kitten. 'Oh, you darling!' cried Sheila. She hugged the creature close and jumped to her feet. The world of beautiful pretence faded like the merest dream. This was real; this was warm and breathing. She ran homeward a few steps and then paused again to examine with ecstasy this new and most wonderful treasure. The kitten's warm purring softness set little shudders of delight running over her body. 'It's alive,' she whispered to herself. 'It's alive!' Quite unexpectedly there flashed into her mind a vision of Aunt Hester's hungry eyes and trembling lips; and now in a vague dim way she understood something of their meaning. Tears for Aunt Hester quivered on her long lashes.

4

The kitten was a great success. Even Sheila's truancy was forgotten in the excitement of greeting this new member of the household. For no one dared to doubt, in the face of Sheila's delight, that the kitten had come to stay. The enthusiasm with which it lapped up a saucerful of milk moved Aunt Hester to declare that the poor little thing was starving, and she was eager to accept its prettiness as an earnest of good behaviour. Sheila, in spite of protests both from Aunt Hester and from the kitten itself, insisted on sprinkling a few drops of water on the creature's nose in witness of the fact that it was to be known henceforward as Tommy. Uncle Peter promised to provide two pennyworth of catsmeat as a christening gift.

Having watched the kitten's antics for five minutes, Uncle Peter remarked that he wouldn't be back to supper.

Hester's happiness evaporated visibly. Her face became a mask. 'Very well, Peter,' she said, in a dull tone. 'You have your key, I expect.'

'Yes, thanks.' Uncle Peter was desperately cheerful. 'Wouldn't do to forget that and have to knock you all up, hey!' He tried to be amused by the idea. 'Well, so long!' he said, pausing at the door.

Going to bed was a dismal affair after so much excitement, chiefly because Aunt Hester was preoccupied with thoughts of her own. 'God bless Granny and Aunt Hester and Uncle Peter and Father and Tommy and me and make me a good girl Amen,' said Sheila, running her words into one enormous polysyllable; and Aunt Hester, the overseer of prayer, did not rebuke her for her unseemly speed.

'Isn't he a dear!' said Sheila, in a last attempt to make conversation before the candle was blown out. 'Don't *you* think he's a dear, auntie?'

5

Next morning, at breakfast, Uncle Peter seemed at once shamefaced and happy. As for Aunt Hester, she kept up a creditable show of gaiety. 'When are you going to tell Granny?' she asked him.

Peter blushed. 'Oh, I don't know,' he said, in an offhand way. '*You* tell her, Hester.'

'Very well.' Hester smiled. 'Sheila and I will tell her after breakfast. You'll be busy to-day, I expect?'

'Bit of shopping,' he confessed, with the air of one caught with his hand in somebody's till.

'Ah, I thought so.'

So, when Uncle Peter had run off to catch the ten eighteen for town, Hester and Sheila went hand-in-hand to knock at Granny's door. The knock was the merest formality, a hollow ritual, for Granny seldom heard knocks at the door and never, even if she heard them, responded. Having knocked, they entered timidly, Sheila trying to hide behind Hester's skirts.

'Some news for you, Granny.'

'Eh?' queried the old woman.

'News for you, Granny.'

'I'm too old for news, my child. . . . There, don't stand like a great gaby, keeping me in suspense. If he's dead tell me so at once, and be off with you. I shall be the next to go. Poor Peter, he never was a strong lad.'

'No one's dead. It's good news. About Peter.'

She imparted her good news about Peter.

'Eh!' muttered Granny. 'Nonsense! He's only a boy!'

'Aren't you pleased, Granny?'

'What a tale!' sniffed the ancient, scornfully. 'When is my glass of milk coming, Hester?'

The glass of milk provided, Aunt Hester, on whom a strange silence had fallen, wandered into the garden still gripping Sheila's hand. They walked up and down the gravel paths, gravely meditating, and finally, at Sheila's request, they entered the kitchen-garden to pay homage to the kingly sunflowers. At sight of them Aunt Hester became rigid, a woman of stone. 'Fetch me the garden scissors, dear. They're in the tool-shed.'

Sheila ran willingly to do her aunt's bidding. But the scissors were hard to find, and she returned to Hester's side just in time to see the last of the sunflowers fall. Flaming yellow, the disenchanted kings drooped upon the earth, riven from their roots.

'I shan't want the scissors now, darling. . . . How sticky my fingers are!'

Torn between wonder and grief, Sheila stared up into her companion's face, trying to read the dark enigma written there. 'But Uncle Peter said they should stay,' she wailed.

'I dare say. But he won't mind now. He's going away from us soon to be married.'

Light, dim but unmistakable, dawned in Sheila's mind. 'Never mind, auntie,' she said, with a gush of compassion. 'I'll give you my Tommy if you like.'

Aunt Hester turned away quickly, and ran into the house.

QUEER'S RIVAL

QUEER'S RIVAL

THE events of that last day, said Saunders, I cannot know at first hand : that will be evident to you as soon as I have finished. Something of what I tell you will be conjecture, or, to speak more precisely, a reconstruction of the affair from quite a mass of evidence that I have. You see I am frank : I lay all my cards on the table. And you, in your turn, will allow me some latitude ; you will not interrupt me to ask how I know this, and from whom I learned that. I tell you at once that much of it comes from the man himself, much more from his wife, and not a little from a bulky black book the two hundred pages of which are blackened with tiny spidery writing, the journal of Samuel Queer. For the rest you must permit me to usurp your function of novelist. I am not sure that the imaginative reconstruction of history does not approach nearer to the spirit of truth than any arid official record can do. Anyhow, I'm going to risk it.

They were an unusual couple from the very first, and their association with each other confirmed their eccentricities. The story of their wooing must be told first, for the sake of the light it throws upon the characters of both, but especially on that of the woman. In those days Emily Dowson, afterwards Mrs Samuel Queer, was an extremely seductive girl in her own subtle way. Never pretty, nor in any conventional sense beautiful, you might easily have failed to look at her twice. If however you did look twice, you stayed looking, if I may put it crudely. She had a flattish nose, plump cheeks, large dark eyes, and an olive complexion. Her hair, which she parted in the middle in the prim fashion of our mothers' time, was wispy, pale brown, and without sheen. Her figure you would perhaps have called dumpy; she was rather under medium height. Altogether a somewhat homely body; and yet her presence, for any sensitive man or woman, was oddly exciting. In spite of her homeliness and her placid manners one felt that she was not what she seemed; that her person was a cunning hieroglyphic in which was written a mystery; that her gentle remarks about the weather, her way of handling a teacup, were part of a symbolism that concealed from the profane, and revealed to the seer, a secret of which she herself was scarcely conscious. She was not, in those days, the mystagogue she afterwards became ; the puerilities of modern spiritualism had not touched her ; she was not histrionic. She had power, but she was unconscious of it. She had not learned then to exploit her mystery, as a child at a certain displeasing stage of its development learns to exploit its immature and hitherto ingenuous fancies. She was, indeed, moving about in worlds not realised. She had all the average half-educated woman's stock of chatter, and only her eyes—dark windows veiling infinite distances—belied the banalities that her lips uttered.

I am speaking of a time when Emily Dowson was in her early twenties. Queer was a few years younger : an untidy, over-sedentary, excessively silent man, even then. Indeed he grossly overdid his taciturnity : it defeated his own ends by drawing attention to itself. He had already that bagginess of the cheek which we associate with elderly justices. Every time he looked at you, which was fortunately seldom enough, you felt like a convicted felon about to receive sentence of death. He was not fat, although he may once have been so. Very early in life he must have developed that slight stoop, and the forward posture of the head that made his clothes hang vilely on him and exposed to view his back collar-stud. He impressed even casual observers as having a skin too large for his frame. It was as if he had stepped into another man's by mistake. He was a sheep in wolf's clothing. For a reserved man, of such odd personal appearance, silence was the very worst policy. If he had taken care to lay in a stock of polite conversation, as Emily had done, he might have passed unnoticed. A silent freak is more conspicuous than a loquacious one, and that is the sole reason why I, when I chanced to meet him at a dinner-party just before I was ordained, marked him down as a specimen worth remembering.

By the merest chance I was a guest under the same roof with them when Queer and Miss Dowson reached the first crisis of their relationship. It was at the dinner-party that I have mentioned. We, with a dozen or so more, were being entertained by a Mrs Durrant, a distant relative of my own whom you have never heard of before and who is negligible so far as this story is concerned. She had never before met Samuel Queer: he owed his place at her board solely to his having just betrothed himself to her niece, Winifred Durrant. It was not what is called a good match;

nor was it a bad one; it was accepted by the world with a politeness that masked indifference tempered by mild surprise. Surprise for which there was every justification. That Queer should be human enough to wish for marriage was only one degree less astonishing than that anybody should have wished to marry him. And, of all unlikely people, Winifred Durrant, a rather pretty girl with plenty of admirers and a real talent for flirtation. This, no doubt, was the kind of talk that went on behind the backs of the affianced pair, and very superficial it was, I dare say. After all, we knew nothing of the man; and the fact that he appeared to be always brooding on the subject of his next Civil Service examination did not necessarily disqualify him as a lover. Anyhow, Winifred didn't think so. She was radiant, and throughout that dinner her eyes glanced across the table at Samuel with a frequency that made indulgent people smile.

Her glances met with no response from Queer, though any other man in the world might have been glad of them. Queer sat walled round by the silence, the almost aggressive silence, that emanated from his personality. Next him was Emily Dowson, talkative as usual, and on her other side was I. To everything she said he listened with a profound attention that would have seemed to me ironical had I not been visited by the curious sense that he was listening, not to her words, but to some subtle undertones of significance to which I myself was deaf. For I, too, was aware of something unusual in Emily Dowson.

After dinner some of the guests wandered away into the garden, among them Queer and his pretty fiancée. I stayed behind, with Emily and some others, to listen to Mrs Durrant's rendering of Chopin. She had just finished playing the Berçeuse with exquisite feeling when I happened to glance at Emily. And I swear to you that I have never seen a human face so transfigured. Those great dark eyes were alight with a rapture of tenderness. And, as I stared, the lids fluttered down, to veil the splendour. The girl trembled, and her rigid form relaxed with extraordinary grace.

I was alarmed by her pallor. For a moment I thought she had fainted. I leaned forward and touched her knee. 'Are you ill, Miss Dowson?' Without opening her eyes, 'No, no,' she said. 'Ask Mrs Durrant to play again for us.' The incident passed unnoticed by the other guests. Mrs Durrant played again. And for fifteen years I supposed the beauty of Chopin's Berçeuse to have been the cause of Emily's ecstasy. It was Queer's journal that put me right.

Queer had accompanied Winifred into the garden with the definite and honourable intention of forgetting the girl whose mysterious power had subjugated him during dinner. But the endeavour was futile. Winifred's prettiness palled on him. The beauty of the summer evening, the busy stillness of nature, the colours of a benign sky : these were tasteless to his drugged senses. He raged inwardly at himself, fretting against the bars of his obsession ; but, rage as he might, he could not get the subtle sweetness of Emily out of his consciousness. He wanted nothing in the world but her ; without her all the world was poison. At last, with a fierce resolve of fidelity, he began to lash himself into a fever of affection for poor Winifred. She had never known him so demonstrative. He whispered passionate words to her ; poured out on her altar the love that was Emily's ; and finally, when for a moment they were hidden from sight of the others, he seized her in his arms and kissed her lips ardently. But it all availed him nothing. The man was spellbound, and no fury of his could break the spell. Presently, to Winifred's chagrin, he abandoned love-making with a sigh and retired into himself. They sauntered back to the house.

Leaving Winifred in the drawing-room, Queer, with no word of apology or explanation, went straight to the library. Like a man in the grip of a demon he snatched at a book, opened it, and began reading. By a prodigious effort of concentration he succeeded in understanding three sentences. Never had he been so angry and so afraid. He, of all men the most self-contained and the least impressionable, was being tormented by love. It was as if, like Hippolytus, he had blasphemed the Cyprian and was being visited with her terrible vengeance. His love for Winifred was a reasonable and orderly emotion. She was charming, and not unintelligent ; but, best of all, she was malleable ; she would be quick to learn his ways and to adapt her own to them. Beyond this he had a genuine brotherly affection for the girl, which, together with a punctilious sense of honour, made it impossible for him to entertain the idea of breaking his engagement. Silently he stormed at himself to this effect, and even as he did so the door opened and Emily herself came into the room. She closed the door behind her but did not advance towards him. Her manner made him stare. 'I want to speak to you,' she said.

As if bereft of speech he bowed his head consentingly.

'Do you believe in marriage without love?' she asked.

'I don't understand you.'

'I think you do,' said Emily, with an air of accusing him. 'Don't you realise that you'll make all three of us unhappy if you marry Winifred Durrant?'

He was pale and trembling at the magnitude of the temptation to take her into his arms.

'How do you know I love you?' he asked, after a pause.

'I have known,' said Emily, 'ever since you kissed me, ten minutes ago.'

2

If that was not a marriage of true minds, said Saunders rather wistfully, surely there never was one. I don't mean that it was a bloodless marriage. Nothing so despicable. They were as fierce and ardent as young love should be. But I must confess to a feeling of almost personal disappointment when I reflect that the marvellous impact of that coming together, the lightning flash of that revelation, was but the prelude to a gradual disenchantment. It's idle to try to apportion blame, the most presumptuous and futile of all endeavours. We live according to our lights, and if our lights are dim whose is the fault? Nor can I trace in detail the history of those years that followed. There is a gap in my record which I can only fill in from hints afforded me in intimate conversation with one or another of the persons of the drama. For a decade or more I lost touch with them. I had been the merest acquaintance, and naturally they saw but little more of me. Finally chance sent them back into my line of vision. Circumstances led them both to make something of a confidant of me. As you know, my position lends me to that kind of thing. I became useful to them as a safety-valve, though not until it was too late did I learn the essential facts in the light of which I might have helped them to a better understanding. Queer was always a little shamefaced when he ventured the least hint of a complaint about his wife (and I liked him the better for that); and as for her, she tolerated me solely, so far as I could see, in order to make a convert of me. She seemed to have drifted out of sympathy with her husband. Ghosts absorbed the most of her attention. 'Discarnate intelligences' she used to call them, but judging from their conversation, which she was good enough to report to me, I thought the substantive inaccurate. She was by now an altogether different woman from the simple, unaffected, unsophisticated soul that I had watched with so much interest at that fateful dinner-party. Commerce with spirits had not improved her. Her intuitions were no longer the spontaneous flashes they had once been. She had become self-conscious, almost complacent. She knew herself to be an extraordinary woman, and the knowledge was fatal to her charm. Powers of a remarkable kind she did undoubtedly possess, clairvoyance, psychometry, and so on ; but whereas at first she had been content to exercise them rarely, almost unwittingly, she now marketed them, not for cash indeed, but for admiration, for the tribute of wonder. She laboured to impress, and she acquired the pretentious vocabulary employed by all mystical charlatans. I really believe that it was by way of reaction from her auras and astrals that I took to smoking strong shag.

Queer himself was angrily intolerant of her ways of thought, her unbridled fancy, her indiscriminate enthusiasms. He complained, very justly, that she lacked intellectual ballast;

and they both, sad to say, lacked humour. Most of all he hated the friends, the soulful chattering friends with whom she wallowed in this jargon ; and most of all her friends he detested those who had no visible bodies. I think he felt that there was something indecent in associating so intimately with naked spirits, and I am not sure he wasn't right. He lost his admiration for Mr Gladstone, and gave up reading Shakespeare, because their frequent messages to his wife made it impossible for him to disentangle the spooks from the living men. You laugh ; and so did I when he told me. It was the nearest approach to a joke that his bleak humour permitted him.

The final cleavage between these unhappy people—the final spiritual cleavage, for they had lapsed into celibacy long before—came when on his way to his bedroom Queer paused one night at his wife's door and heard her murmuring passionate endearments in the darkness. 'How soon will you come, my love ? Come soon, come soon !' For one moment, which passed quickly, he was arrested by an incredibly vulgar suspicion. Then, nauseated and revolted, he strode on to his own room, reflecting with what bitterness that he was married to a hysterical fool, and dis-

placed in his wife's affections by a ghost. He
was consumed with jealousy, and overwhelmed
with self-loathing to find that he was capable
of jealousy. He felt contaminated, unclean,
sharing the contamination of his wife. A flesh
and blood rival would have been more welcome
to him. But to be ousted, as it were from his
bed, by a mere figment of an unbalanced fancy !
From that day he treated his wife as though
she were dead. His heart turned to stone.
And as though in revenge upon the life that
had treated him so scurvily he set about
flouting, with great deliberation, all his rigid
moral principles. He drank excessively ; he
drugged himself ; he began that liaison with
the notorious Mrs O'Malley which ultimately
set his name in four-inch letters on half the
evening newspaper placards in London. At
this time Queer was thirty five. No doubt
you remember something of the case. This
Mrs O'Malley obtained against her husband
a decree nisi which the court, on the inter-
vention of the King's Proctor, refused to
make absolute. That was not the worst. The
law chose to ' make an example ' of this poor
silly woman by sentencing her to a short term
for perjury. Queer was one of the several men
whose names figured in both cases,

3

On that last morning of all Samuel Queer rose from his bed feeling a little surprised that he was still alive. Utterly disenchanted with life, he had more than once gone to meet death half-way; but that exalted personage seemed unwilling to make his acquaintance, or perhaps merely indifferent, busy (as he always was) hunting happier men. But if Queer was a little surprised, he was, for once in a way, not disappointed. He felt more at peace with the world, as though in his dreams he had shaken off his customary tormenting thoughts. His bed was situated in a little alcove of the room and hidden by green curtains, for it was the man's fancy to sleep in the presence of his books (he had been a great reader in his more equable days), and in the leisure of the daytime he used this same room as a study or library. Often, indeed, when he could avoid his wife in no other way, he had his meals brought up to him. And so this morning, with a lighter step than usual, he slipped between the curtains into the heartening presence of the only friends that remained to him. They lined the walls, neither rejecting nor importuning him, but waiting his pleasure in mute fidelity. While he quickly dressed he looked round at these books with satisfaction; and finally, his toilet complete, he slipped a dainty Sir Thomas Browne into his pocket and ran downstairs and out of the house. No one saw him go.

He must have risen early and walked at a good pace, for eleven o'clock found him some twenty miles across country entering the cottage in which, on her release from prison, he had taken care to instal Mrs O'Malley. He found her in her little back garden staring wistfully at the great belt of pinewoods that shut off the horizon from her vision. It was their first meeting since the day of her release. She did not rise to greet him. She merely turned eyes of anguish upon him and sat still. He, on his part, did not attempt to touch her. Instead, he stood three yards away and set himself to charm away her sad humour by talk of the happy future he proposed for them both. ' My darling girl, we'll go away somewhere abroad and make a new start. We'll get this damned police-court taste out of our mouths and be simple married people.' He began improvising plans with great fluency. Hitherto he had been bound to his home and his wife by ties of honour, respectability, and so on. He had felt it his duty to remain a Civil Servant, seeing no other way of earning his bread. He had been reluctant to leave his wife, even though he detested her, to manage on her meagre eighty or ninety pounds a year, which was all her private income. But now, he said, he was determined. With his 'darling girl' he would cut right adrift from that bleak existence, that hypocritical keeping up of appearances; and they would run off to some colony together and live happily ever after. He was lyrical and rather childlike in his enthusiasm. But Mrs O'Malley seemed lost in despondency. To all his protestations she could only repeat, with a half-sob, 'Please go away. Please go away. Some other time, perhaps, we'll talk it over.'

Repulsed, then, but not, I think, disheartened, Queer turned back home. And on the way a curious thing happened to him, a change of heart and—which is more to the present point—a change of mind. Somehow he forgot that his wife no longer cared for him, forgot that he himself loathed and despised his wife. There settled upon his consciousness—or so my fancy suggests—the intoxicating idea that he was returning, hastening after a long absence, to the arms of his beloved.

He reached the door of his house soon after I had quitted it. Mrs Queer had sent for me during the morning, and I had just left her after a long and troubled conference. From her own lips, next day, I heard the incredible conclusion of the whole matter.

Queer ran upstairs like a light-hearted boy, his feet scarcely touching ground. At the stairhead his wife waited with glowing eyes for her lover. She saw him, was illuminated with joy, and opened her arms to enfold him. ' Ah, my dear love, you have come to me at last, and my eyes see you ! ' They clung together for a moment of rapture. Then he gently disengaged himself from her embrace and moved on towards his own room.

' Not there ! ' she pleaded. ' Don't go there. You, you are my husband.'

But her request seemed only to make him the more determined to go there. He resolutely opened the door, and she followed, grey with fear.

Without a word he stepped across the room and drew back the curtains that concealed his bed. He made one gesture of horror, seeing prone before him the corpse of Samuel Queer. Then, with a strange deliberation, he flung himself upon the bed. Emily looked, for one mad moment, upon those two grotesque bed-fellows, identical in every feature like a pair of middle-aged twins. With a dry gasp of agony she hid her face in her hands. And when she dared to look again, there was only the one white face of death upon that pillow.

THE DARK HOUSE

THE DARK HOUSE

I HAD been in the railway carriage for nearly six hours, passing through country bleak and unfamiliar, before my seedy little fellow-traveller made up his mind to speak to me. He was a shortish, square-faced man, with a little sharp nose and russet side-whiskers. Silky black hair was plastered thinly across his bald crown.

'Might one enquire how far you were thinking of travelling, sir?'

When I named my destination, the fellow rubbed his hands in delight. 'Why, sir, that's where I am alighting, if it isn't taking a liberty. How small the world is, after all! I haven't the pleasure of knowing your name, sir; but mine is Mr Dolphin. Albert Edward Dolphin, sir, named after His late Majesty.'

I did not at once indulge Mr Dolphin in the pleasure of knowing my name, but he was not discouraged.

'You put me in mind, sir, of a certain young gentleman, a university gentleman, that is coming to assist the Countess with her English correspondence, she being a Spanish lady, sir, but busy with charitable work for our gallant seamen. Not that I've seen the gentleman, and yet you put me in mind of him, if I make my meaning clear.'

'Was his name Pendelling?' I asked, with a friendly grin. 'And did he answer an advertisement in *The Times*?'

'Can it be, sir,' cried my companion, 'that you . . . ?'

'It can. It is. And you . . .'

'I am Her Ladyship's butler, sir.'

'You have been on your holiday, no doubt?'

'A brief respite, sir,' he said. 'A brief respite. But had I known you were coming to-day, sir, I should have been back to my duty yesterday.' His expression became one of tragical anxiety. 'Dear me!' he exclaimed. 'Dearie, dearie me! Why, I hardly know, sir, who will come to meet you, me being not available for that purpose, which it would have been a privilege, I'm sure. Five miles from the station it is, sir, and a very old-fashioned five miles at that, as the saying is. It would *hardly* do, I think, to have to walk five miles on a night like this.'

'But surely,' I protested, 'there is some one else they could send!'

'Never one,' said Mr Dolphin with relish, scarcely troubling to conceal his enjoyment of my anxiety. 'We don't keep a large staff, sir. There's myself and young Hogg, and sometimes, sometimes I say, there's a kitchen-maid. Young Hogg isn't good for much. In fact, I would be telling you a lie, sir, if I said young Hogg was quite steady in the upper storey. It's a small household, you see ; and unless His Highness himself should take the fancy to come, why it will be Shanks's pony for the two of us, sir, and as long and dark a road as ever a man was murdered on.'

'His Highness ! ' I echoed. ' What highness is this ? "

'His Highness the Baron,' said Mr Dolphin, his tone rich with obsequiousness.

' What baron ? '

'Why, sir,' said Mr Dolphin in surprise, '*the* Baron ! There's only one Baron. Her Ladyship's stepson, so to speak. A youngish gentleman, sir, but very little younger than Her Ladyship herself.' His eye shone unpleasantly. ' But *Honi soit*, sir, as the saying is. And I'm sure that a nicer-spoken lady and gentleman doesn't step the earth, foreigners and all though they *may* be. It's always " Please, Dolphin ! " and " Thank you, Dolphin!" with them, sir, whether in sunshine or rain, as one might say.'

Mr Dolphin continued to prattle until we reached our station. Then, briskly transformed into the perfect manservant, he mutely insisted on carrying my bag and in keeping a pace or two behind me, like a dog. He was the embodiment of mute respect. As we stepped on to the platform I heard a reverential whisper behind me: 'His Highness!'; and a tall figure stepped out of the shadows to greet me.

Mist-shrouded light from the one lamp the little station boasted fell across the Baron's face as he advanced towards me. Most of him was in strong shadow, and the proportion between light and shade changed with every step he took. The effect was a series of flashing pictures, a liquid apparition. The confusion endured but for an instant. I found myself grasping a large hairy hand, and responding to a courteous greeting. The Baron's articulation and choice of words were foreign in their precision, but there was scarcely a trace of accent. His voice, like the man himself, was big and vigorously masculine.

'Have I the pleasure,' he said, 'of meeting Mr Pendelling?' Waiting for no reply, he added: 'I hope the long journey has not been too fatiguing?'

'Well, no,' I assured him politely, but without enthusiasm. 'But I'm not sorry to have done with it.'

At this I heard behind me a whispered titter, instantly smothered by a short rasping cough. At this reminder of Mr Dolphin's proximity the newly kindled warmth died out of me. But now the Baron was leading the way out of the station. At the barrier an undersized man pounced upon us to demand tickets; he took them greedily, as though they had been good to eat and he distracted with hunger. In the station yard, awaiting us, was a black shape that presently resolved itself into a dogcart. The mottled horse flashed a malevolent eye upon me as I stumbled towards him, and bared his teeth in a kind of grin. Mr Dolphin, having hoisted up my luggage and his own, climbed nimbly into the driver's seat and gathered the reins into his chubby fingers. The Baron and I settled down, each with a rug on our knees, and the dogcart moved off into the velvet night. Velvet at first, I thought, but afterwards harder and more hostile. The candle-lamps we carried served only to make visible the neighbouring darkness. Huddled in my great coat, buttoned up to the ears yet chilled to the bone, I watched the curious lolloping movement of the horse, his haunches swaying laterally, his head with its twitching ears moving up and down, the whole unreal spectacle suggesting his imminent disintegration. Situated as I was, a trick of perspective rendered to me this equine phenomenon as a mass of heaving matter singularly unmeaning and disorganic; but I was able to discern with some faint pleasure the rhythm of beating hooves. When my eyes wandered it was only to encounter the impenetrable blackness. With neither moon nor star visible, with no light at all except the uneasy pallor cast by our lamps upon the black receding wall that faced us, I felt as though we were in the bowels of a universal mine that might at any moment, with a sudden terrible magnifying of its growling noises, crash in upon us.

Half an hour brought us to the journey's end. The dogcart, dangerously swerving, turned into what I judged to be a cobbled courtyard. Dimly I made out the shapes of stables and other outbuildings, and, facing us, a long low house with two red windows faintly glowing a welcome.

'Your horse will be glad to turn in,' I remarked, for the sake of saying something.

'Dolphin will see to that,' returned the

Baron. 'Come along, Mr Pendelling. You'll have to pick your way. The yard is full of puddles.'

Full of puddles it was, and, being invisible on such a night as this, they were not to be avoided. Past caring for such minor discomforts now that I was within sight of haven, I splashed cheerfully enough in the Baron's wake. He stepped up to the front door, which opened at his touch. With a murmured apology he preceded me into the dark hall, and stood there cursing volubly. He stamped up and down, his boots making a sharp sound on the tiled floor. 'Where in thunder is that Hogg?' he was muttering. He spoke in his own language, but the word Hogg did not seem German, and an instant later I recognised it as the name that Mr Dolphin had mentioned to me. There followed a furious silence, while the Baron seemed to be fumbling in his pockets—for matches, as I supposed. Then he gave vent to a tremendous roar, which the lofty hall sent back to him in ghostly echoes. At first I feared that this echoing mockery was to be the only response that the dark house would vouchsafe us, and it was not only the physical discomfort of my chill damp clothes that made me shiver a little. But soon we heard the shuffle of approaching feet. Somewhere, at the end of a long corridor, a door opened, and in the doorway a flickering candle wavered towards us. The light at first dazzled my unaccustomed eyes, but when I could discern the shape and features of the candle-bearer I saw him to be a rawboned, ungainly lad, shock-headed, with a long equine face and timid foolish eyes.

'So!' said the Baron. 'Why are there no lights in this place, Master Hogg?'

The fellow stopped dead in his march. He stared sulkily from one of us to the other, but made no reply. The Baron, controlling his anger, did not repeat his question, but, in a gentler tone, put another in its stead.

'Now, Hogg, listen to me. This is Mr Pendelling. Do you know which room Mr Pendelling is to occupy?'

Hogg favoured me with a broad grin, and nodded slyly.

'You are sure?' persisted his master.

'Ay, Baron.'

'Then take Mr Pendelling's bag, and shew him the way upstairs.'

Retaining my bag, which he shewed no eagerness to relieve me of, I followed the halfwit up a broad oak stairway, along a passage, and into a low-ceiled room that contained a large four-poster bed, ancient and canopied.

Hogg placed the candlestick on the extreme edge of the wash-stand, from which it immediately fell to the floor. The light was extinguished; we were alone in utter darkness. Braced to meet this new discomfort, I stood very still, listening. My companion was completely hidden from me; nor could I hear him move or breathe. Without haste, rather with a certain deliberation, I struck a match; in whose light I could then discern him, an arm's-length distant, regarding me with the pathetic gravity of a cow. The candle relit, we exchanged a long steady stare. I felt for him nothing but compassion, together with that stirring of affection which compassion implies. It was as if I looked into the eyes of some poor dumb creature who, if he could, would tell me much. Witless perhaps he was, but innocent; dull and foolish, but fundamentally sane. What catastrophe, I wondered, had deprived him of the full use of his wits? For a moment, as our eyes communed, I was in hope of receiving an answer to my unspoken question; but even as the hope was born a vague grin spread over the face of him who alone could fulfil it.

When I had washed and changed, I made my way back to the hall, which was now lit by three candles and peopled with lurking shadows.

The Baron emerged from a doorway to my right and invited me to come and get warm.

'I am sure you must be tired,' he said, 'and ready for a meal.' He conducted me into a long low room, divided by a curtain into two parts. A log-fire blazed on the open hearth, and this was the only illumination. It sufficed, however, to make visible the satin sheen of walls papered in old gold, the heavy oak furniture, and a black divan on which a woman was reclining. 'Yes,' said the Baron, heavily humorous. 'The outer man is cold, I expect, and the inner man is empty. Come, let us fill him.'

At my entry the woman rose to greet me. The Baron, with some pomp, pronounced an introduction. The Countess bowed, gracefully and graciously, but without extending her hand. I responded with such ceremony as I was master of : which was not much, perhaps, for I was conscious of standing face to face with the woman—the young Spanish widow of a German count—whose odd advertisement I had answered. With all the romantic fire of my twenty five years I had conceived her as a lovely creature ; and here was my dream in being. I cannot say that she fulfilled the dream : rather she displaced it, substituting, for a conventional beauty of form and feature and colouring, some subtle charm, indefinable and unmistakable as a perfume, that made one's habitual standards seem of no account. In person she was fragile, unsubstantial as gossamer, of medium stature, simply attired. This was my first impression, an impression of exquisite ethereality. She possessed, for my astonished eyes, at once the perfection of art and the enchanting bloom of young breathing life. I saw her, as I see every lovely living thing, against a background of the ultimate doom that encompasses all humanity ; and if our eyes met for an instant, and rested in brief communion, I think that in mine there must have been visible some hint of a dawning emotion that was soon to flood my world with tragic lightning. Her face was a perfect oval, sallow rather than olive, a sallowness only redeemed—but how generously !—by the roseflush of the cheeks. These particulars I scarcely noticed at this first encounter, lost as I was in the dark lustrous world of her eyes. It was a world quick with inexhaustible beauty and dark with an enigma that a man might willingly cast away his life in despair of solving. And I knew, not then but days later, in the quiet of my bed, that it was a world in which I must dwell, in which I must travel and adventure, in which I must lose myself, or be for ever lost.

Speaking English with difficulty, she faltered half-timidly some conventional greeting. I murmured a reply, and we all, the Baron leading, turned towards the damask curtains. Had some one called us? I had heard nothing, but instinctively we three had turned. In the middle of the curtain, gaily regarding me, was a human face. It seemed to hang there, trunkless, having all the air of being amused by its own decapitation. My involuntary start passed unnoticed, except perhaps by Mr Dolphin himself, who now, fully revealing himself, pulled the curtains apart and announced supper.

During supper I made opportunities of covertly examining my new acquaintances, and more than once, to my chagrin, Mr Dolphin, who waited on us too zealously, caught me in the act. On such occasions his elaborately concealed smile, his air of sharing a secret with me, was little short of insulting. I ignored these evidences of ill-breeding as best I could, and exercised more discretion in my scrutiny of my host and hostess. The contrast between the two was almost grotesque; she scarce solid enough for mortality, a visible fragrance, a flower's breath, a miracle of music wrought in perishable flesh ; and he a great lump of a man, with round face, broad nostrils, bristling moustache, and a mass of black hair that started up from his head as though in alarm. It seemed incredible that beings so remote from each other could exist in the same universe. Mr Dolphin had not erred in saying that the Countess was but little older than her stepson. I could easily have believed her younger.

Conversation, what there was of it, ran on customary lines. The Baron talked most—of my journey, of university life, of military service—and I did my best, by seconding his efforts, to conceal the straying of my thoughts. The Countess said little, the language, I supposed, proving too troublesome for her ; but despite her silence and stillness she remained for me the only reality in a world of phantoms. Flowerlike, delicately breasted, she created for me with every breath she took, with every little indolent movement of her hands, a new world of dazzling conjecture.

'The storm is rising,' I said.

From my contemplation of ideal beauty I had returned with a start to the actual world, to the black night that howled about us, to this little lit room suspended, a forlorn beacon, in the illimitable environing void. The wind now was gathering violence, coming in great gusts that, in my fancy, threatened us all with destruction. I caught myself waiting for its approach, as a spent swimmer might wait, sick with fear, for some immense wall of water reared against the sky to crash down upon him. Every gust was followed by a breathless silence broken only by distant wailing. My companions took no notice of this clamour.

'Do you often have such storms as this?' I asked, raising my voice above the din.

It was to the Countess that I addressed my question, but the Baron took it up, forcing me in mere politeness to turn in his direction.

'You must understand . . .'

So he began, and then stopped speaking, his mouth partly open, the expression of his face unchanged. I became aware of a silence that was absolute, silence and stillness more terrible than that of death. There was now no wind. The clock, whose ticking I had not consciously noticed, made no sound. The burbling noise of the wood-fire had ceased. Without turning my head I was aware of the Countess, rigid as stone, and of Dolphin, bending deferentially towards her, stiff, motionless, unbreathing. It was as if the everlasting flux had been arrested. We were fixed and held fast, all four of us, in a frozen moment.

I listened for my own heart's beat, and heard nothing, except a voice that said :

'. . . Mr Pendelling, that we are in a very exposed position here. There are no houses to break the wind for miles round.'

It was the Baron completing his sentence. Life flowed on as before. I looked in dismay from face to face, seeking for evidence there of some such fear as gripped myself. But they were all serenely unconscious of anything unusual. The storm had resumed its clamour ; and I knew myself once more for what I was and had always been, a pilgrim in an alien world.

2

Not all the storms in the world could have kept me awake that night. I fell asleep as soon as my limbs were relaxed in the soft caress of that feather-bed, and I slept dreamlessly till morning. Even the insinuating voice of Mr Dolphin, telling me that my hot water was at the door, caused in me no renewal of distaste. The blessed oblivion that had intervened since last night had purged me of terrors. It had given a chance, too, for the sceptic in me to reassert himself. All that queerness, those disconcerting intimations of an enveloping darkness, had it been all but a trick of the nerves ? Could mere physical discomfort weave such fantasies ? I did not bother to answer these questions, being content with the knowledge that to have asked them was a symptom of mental health. I went to the window and looked out, eager for my first sight of the Countess's demesne.

The day was very fair, and the garden upon which I looked was beautiful even in winter and neglect. It stretched away from me in a series of three graduated lawns, the remotest and highest of which was enclosed on three sides by tall pines. Leaning out of the window I saw with delighted surprise that on each side of the estate ran a broad river, and it pleased me to suppose that somewhere just beyond that belt of pines the two travellers met in a mighty confluence of waters. I dressed in haste and set out in search of the waterfall whose voice I fancied I could already hear. By following the little moss-grown flagged path, by ascending two sets of stone steps and traversing the pine-copse, I at last found it. The scene was wonderfully unreal. Never had I seen so ancient and so beautiful a desolation. I stood on an iron bridge and filled my senses with the forlorn strangeness of it all. Where the two rivers met the broad water flowed gently over a succession of wide stone terraces that hinted to my imagination a buried city. At my feet, under the bridge, the river plunged deeply, a living green wall of water ending in furious foam, to find at last a meditative quietude in the great lake beyond. On this lake, as upon a mirror, sailed superb swans, symbols to me of a fabulous antiquity ; and others on the incredible white terraces, where the water spread a gleaming film, stood, still as images and no more real than their reflections, or gently fluttered from step to step arching proudly their elegant necks. They were the only living things in a region that seemed to have been deserted for ten thousand years.

I stood so long at gaze, turning over my dreams, that when presently I woke to a sense of time I was alarmed lest I should be late for breakfast. My fear was unfounded, for when I entered the house the Baron had only just come downstairs. We took our meal alone, the Baron explaining that his stepmother lived an extremely secluded life and seldom emerged from her privacy until evening. After breakfast he instructed me in my secretarial duties. These were ridiculously light. There were a few letters to be acknowledged, a few accounts to be looked into, and that was all. By lunchtime my work was over for the day, and I had nothing to do but roam, with my golden thoughts for company, the giant hills by which we were surrounded. They were splendid and rather terrible, these hills, in their winter nakedness ; their great limbs seemed to sprawl in the sky with violent masculine gestures. In their laps lay tarns of dark clear water, ominously still ; at their feet, linking with a silver cord one with another, stretched the long lake into which our two rivers ran.

One day of this strange new life was like another, and all were darkly glistening with a significance that I could but dimly read. In the evenings we three sat together in the firelight, the Baron in one corner, a tiny reading lamp focussed on his book, the Countess and I at the hearth talking in undertones with long intervals of eloquent silence. It was the undertones, the undertones of meaning and emotion, that invested with such surpassing value the often trivial remarks that we exchanged. I felt that but for the barrier of language we should have achieved in our first half-hour a marvellous intimacy. She had little or no English ; and not only was my German inadequate, but whenever I ventured to use it she shook her head with an enigmatic smile. In her own tongue, smooth and lyrical as running water, I could not follow her, though I often urged her to speak it, so magically did it enhance the beauty of her soft, hesitating voice. For the most part we struggled along with English, she in rare brief sentences, I at greater length ; and while I talked I looked into her deep, dark, listening eyes, which were wistful with the endeavour to understand. We talked, for the most part, of English poetry, in which she was well read, and of religion, with occasional excursions into regions more mundane, for her interests were surprisingly various. She told me, perhaps in jest, that an ancestor of hers had perished with the Great Armada, an idea that intoxicated me with an utterly boyish pleasure. Our meagre but enormously protracted dialogues would gain nothing, and lose all their delicate bloom, by being written down. Indeed, what we said does not and did not matter ; for again and again I was visited by the joyous intuition that the words we uttered, intellectually of so small account, were but the external mechanism of a more vital interchange, and all our linguistic impediments the mere surface friction that generated an inward illumination intimately shared.

My long afternoon rambles among hills became part of my daily routine, and sometimes the Baron accompanied me. In general he was a morose, phlegmatic man ; but on these occasions, intoxicated with the mountain air, he would exhibit a melancholy soulfulness that proved an excellent foil to my new-found delight, talking volubly—and sometimes in German—of *Weltschmerz* and transcendentalism and the Ideal Woman. At this last phrase I seldom failed to smile with secret pleasure in the knowledge that for me the ideal had become flesh, and that I, day by day, beheld her glory.

It was on one of these excursions that I first saw Eve Richardson.

'Now that is a very fine young woman,' said the Baron, when she had acknowledged our salutes and passed by. He emphasised his verdict by turning to stare at her departing figure, which was, I had to admit, exceedingly comely. Her face, grave, broad-browed, and kindly, lingered in my memory with just enough insistence to make me vaguely resent the Baron's almost stupefied admiration.

'Who is she?' I asked.

'He would be a fortunate fellow,' asserted the Baron, still staring, 'who had so splendid a woman for wife.'

I tried to laugh him out of his obsession. 'My dear Baron, she is probably the most ordinary of country girls. And, anyhow, there are more things in this world than love to think about.'

'So?' said the Baron, with ponderous irony. 'Did your Shakespeare think so? Did your Swinburne?'

He began declaiming Swinburne at me, with immense earnestness:

> 'Loff, that is feerst and last of all things made,
> The light that hass the living woorld for shade,
> The spirit that for temporal veil hass on
> The souls of ulla men wofen in unison,
> One fiery raiment with all lives inwrought
> And lights——'

But here I interrupted him with a plea for mercy. The effect of English verse on his speech was extraordinary. It brought out all the Teuton in him. He mouthed it with strange grimaces and a barbaric accent. At my grinning protest he stopped short and scowled at me darkly.

'Ah, you laugh at me, *nicht wahr*? I am the butt for you, yes? Come now, what must I do to you? Must I flog you with my nice great stick?' His eyebrows bristled fiercely. I stared in surprise. 'No, no, no, no,' he went on, with sudden sunshine breaking over his face. 'I shall not hurt you, my little Pendelling. We are stout friends ever.'

Thereupon he resumed at once his masterly

imitation of the English country gentleman, and told me that the girl we had met was the daughter of a neighbouring yeoman-farmer. He had seen her before ; he was extremely interested in her ; and he had sometimes thought that she would be just the right companion for the poor lonely Countess. The farm, I knew, could not be less than five miles distant. I pictured it as old and spacious, a white stone house heavily thatched, copiously and harmoniously gabled, a day-dream clear and crisp in winter sunlight. I endowed this house with an ideal farmyard, clean and bright and fragrant with vigorous smells ; and little pink pigs, each sweet as a new-washed babe, peered at me from behind their innocent snouts and grunted with pleasure. A grey bitch, big with pregnancy, waddled over the cobblestones, disdainfully ignoring the attentions of my ideal hens. A laden hay-wain rumbled into the yard drawn by two brown and brawny mares. And, in due time, the farmer's daughter, she who had inspired this vision, stepped out of the dairy with a pair of gleaming milk-pails hanging from a yoke on her shoulders. Everything in the picture was as it should be ; nothing could be removed from it (least of all the girl) without serious offence to my notion of what was fitting. A farmer's girl she was, a farmer's girl let her remain. As for the Countess's loneliness, I was not unwilling to alleviate that as best I could. Delicately, choosing my words with care, I tried to express something of this point of view to the Baron. But he flattened it out, in his bovine way, by making no response beyond reiterating his admiration of the girl and his desire to see her a member of his household.

'My poor stepmother will, I am confident, be very pleased with her,' he finished, smiling upon me expansively as though he had not heard a word of my timid objections.

A few days later, by happy chance, I met Eve Richardson again, and within a yard or two of our first meeting-place. This time I was alone, and acting on a sudden impulse I took the bold course of speaking to her, on some trivial pretext or another, in the hope that some word would fall that might give me wind of any developments that promised. The Baron had spent the previous day riding, and it was in my mind that possibly he had already begun his sentimental campaign against the farm. This conjecture proved correct. I asked the girl presently whether she was not afraid to walk alone in country so deserted. She answered me readily enough, smiling pleasantly and without the least hint of coquetry at the notion that there was anything to fear.

'It's not me,' she said, 'that should be afraid.' And her eyes became grave in their scrutiny.

I was at a loss to understand her. 'You mean . . . ?' But part of her meaning was evident. 'You surely can't mean that *I* am in any danger.'

She still gazed in silence, and I had leisure to admire, with the detachment of a man whose heart is elsewhere, her innocent frank gaze, the lovely poise of her head, the bloom and the confident careless grace of her ardent young womanhood. The darkness of her hair, hidden only in part by a little toque-hat, contrasted piquantly with the blue kindliness of her large eyes. I recognised these charms, but they did not stir me, thrall as I was to a more potent enchantment. None the less I liked her well enough to hate the idea of her suffering the attentions of the Baron.

'You can't mean,' I insisted, 'that *I* have anything to fear?'

At this she nodded. 'I know nothing of dangers,' she said, and looked away at last, not sure of how to proceed. 'But I wish you hadn't come.'

I smiled ruefully. 'But why?'

'I don't know why. But you don't seem

to fit down there. It's such a queer house.'

'You mean the people are queer?' I suggested.

'Queer, yes, and . . .' She seemed to be seeking for a more exact word. But her next words confessed failure. 'I don't like them very much. And why you, who are so . . . so very different . . .'

'Isn't it perhaps that you misjudge them?' I said gently. 'At first they struck me, too, as odd. But now that I know them better—why, the Countess is a most charming woman, and even the Baron is not so bad, in his comic way.'

'That Countess!' she exclaimed, under her breath. 'They say such terrible strange things of her. But there!—we can't believe all we hear, can we?'

'What do they say of her?' I demanded, with some indignation.

She became reserved at the first sign of my anger. 'Oh, nothing much. Nothing like that. Are you staying there long, Mr Pendelling?'

'Several weeks,' I said firmly. 'So you know my name?'

'Why, of course!' She smiled once more. 'Everybody knows everything in a country place. I mustn't stop any longer. But . . .'

She hesitated a moment, then pointed in the direction of the next valley. 'That's our farm, over there. If ever you need help I'm sure my father . . .'

As if repenting her rashness, she turned away without finishing her sentence, and hurried towards her home. I did not seek to detain her. I was too puzzled for any decisive action : puzzled not only by her vague hints of danger but by the difficulty of imagining what purpose could have brought her so many miles from home, away from her own village, and why she had seen fit to abandon that purpose.

3

A week later I had another mystery to ponder ; for one day, returning from my accustomed walk, I found Eve Richardson installed in the house as the Countess's companion. The inconsistency between her words and her deeds made me suspect some double dealing, and my response to her cheerful greeting was none too cordial. I did not waste time on her motives, being too absorbed in what had now become the master-purpose of my life. I saw that the presence of another woman, in constant attendance on the Countess, would make my courting impossibly difficult. For courting, of a subtle kind, was now my chief preoccupation. My hopes, keeping pace with my desires, were more arrogant than any I could have dared to entertain a few weeks earlier. To marry the Countess, could I but win her love, seemed no longer a fool's dream. She was exiled, comparatively alone, in need (I flattered myself) of the devotion I could offer, and by no means wealthy. She lived, I plausibly guessed, on the bounty of her stepson—he had hinted as much— and he himself, it appeared, had very limited means. I saw no reason to suppose myself shut out by mere disparity of rank from the paradise I sought to enter. She had confessed, almost with pride, to a comparatively plebeian origin, and made no effort to sustain the outward and visible signs of aristocracy. Her household was ordered without pretence to anything more than solid and simple comfort ; and her thoughts shone like stars in a heaven that knew nothing of social inequalities. Every evening I grew a little more courageous, took a little less care to hide the state of my heart. And now this progress was likely to be interrupted.

Events fulfilled my dismal prophecy. Eve's duties as companion did not begin, as it seemed to me, until seven o'clock in the evening; for the Countess, faithful to her strange rule, never appeared in public until that hour, and during the day the so-called companion was constantly to be seen about the house busied in some domestic task, or strolling in the garden with our sentimental Baron. In the evening she would sit with the rest of us, discreetly distant, but watchful and well within earshot. So gentle were her eyes, even in vigilance, that I could not in my heart accuse her of hostility. Indeed she gave every evidence of wishing to be my friend, making frequent opportunities for a chance word with me. Her bearing on these private occasions was reserved yet curiously maternal. Her smile, I thought, always held a suggestion of solicitude. Once or twice I caught glimpses of a deeper significance. 'I am glad,' she said, 'that you are so different.' This had a flattering sound, and I was not altogether pleased when she immediately explained the flattery away by defining her 'different' as 'not queer, like the others.' It was my jog-trot ordinariness that attracted her. I was safe anchorage in a house that held, for her, perilous possibilities. I asked her to tell me what she imagined these possibilities to be.

'The Countess,' she said. 'There is something about her that frightens me. I can't explain it. If you were to go away, Guy, I couldn't stay here another minute.'

She had never before called me by my first name, and now it had slipped out accidentally. She blushed for the accident, and in confusion added hurriedly : ' Why am I never allowed near her until evening ? And why don't they light their lamps ? '

' I believe you've been indulging your romantic fancy about these harmless people,' I said, smiling. ' Why *should* they light lamps ? For my part, I prefer the firelight.'

It was Eve's coming to the dark house that precipitated the crisis of my wooing. Made desperate by repeated frustration, I resolved to ask the Countess to grant me a private interview somewhere outside the house. Before I had time to cool I put my resolve into effect. Everybody in the room must have heard my agitated request, but for that I was past caring. Eve appeared frankly frightened, and even the Baron, reading in his corner as usual, gave me a startled glance. The Countess alone was apparently quite unmoved, though I found significance in her long hesitation to reply. I waited, almost with breath held. Then, though she did not look up, her hand fluttered towards my own and brushed it in a phantom caress. A falling rose-petal could not have touched me more lightly.

'To-morrow!' I said eagerly.

'In the evening,' she replied in a whisper.

'Before the light fails,' I urged her.

Then she yielded me her marvellous eyes. 'No, my dear. In moonlight.'

'Yes, moonlight,' I echoed, in a very delirium of bliss. 'On the bridge . . . by the lake . . . moonlight.' For several minutes I could not utter another word. The silence between us was quick with a unique emotion.

Next day I despatched what little work there was with even more expedition than usual; and after an early lunch, which Eve Richardson was good enough to prepare specially for me, I set out to do battle, under the open sky, with my rising excitement. Eve, noticing my exultation, could not repress the beginnings of a sorrowful smile as I bade her good day. I guessed that she wished to make some reference to the events of the evening before, and to dissuade me from my heart's desire; but I affected a brisk cheerfulness that made such intimacies impossible. Arrogantly youthful I strode out of the house to brave the enigma of a grey and empty day. The ground was hard with frost, and the sky hard with livid derision of my boundless dreaming. White mist shrouded the tall figures of the brooding hills. The waste grey land gave me no word of invitation. The sound of my own footsteps, and the tapping of my iron-pointed ash stick upon the iron ground, was all that made assault upon the staring silence. My own breath, a visible cloud, preceded me ; and echo, like my own wraith, followed. But these hostilities were impotent against my ardour. The sun was shut out from this strange bleak region of my adventuring, but the rose I cherished in my heart was all-sufficing loveliness. The moon might fail to rise upon my meeting with the beloved, but the moon in my mind would shine with surpassing glory. I was proof to-day against all discouragement. Nature's asperities held no sting for me except the sting of a challenge exultantly accepted. It was the Countess herself who had filled me with the strength of ten men ; yet it was the thought of her that made me, from time to time, catch my breath in alarm at the presumption of the hopes that inflated me. Of herself I could not think without trembling ecstasy. I bowed in adoration of the mystery of her loveliness, a mystery luminously dark, object of unappeasable wonder. Upon her personality, so intimately dear to me yet inexhaustibly enigmatical, I lavished all the radiant dreams, spiritual and sensual, of a belated adolescence. I knew her to be passionate and kind, ingenuous and subtly wise, mistress of a hundred high thoughts beyond reach of my soaring imagination. This much at least I could confidently infer from my brief close contact with her mind. This much the ethereal touch of her hand had taught me. Inspirited by these convictions I strode on and on, mile after mile without weariness, making a circuit of the great, bleak, sunless hills. At Eve's suggestion I had brought a few sandwiches with me ; and, having eaten these, I resolved not to return for tea but to go straight to the appointed place at the appointed hour. Excitement quickened my steps as at last I turned homewards. A wind was rising to disperse the mist from the sky, and I hailed it as a happy omen.

Hours later, when I neared the bridge, I saw with a stab of compunction that she was awaiting me, gloved and cloaked and wearing a wide-brimmed hat. These outdoor clothes, in which I had never before seen her, wonderfully enhanced her seductiveness. She was leaning on the parapet. Her eyes, which were shaded from the meagre moonlight, I could not see ; but her posture suggested that she was lost in reverie. The gliding swans, ghostly-pale upon the lake, were her dim mysterious dreams. The sound of falling water echoed my own heart's tumult.

I ran towards her with eager, penitent steps. 'My dear, am I late? Have you been waiting long?'

'No,' answered her sweet, soft voice, 'you are not late. It is I who am early.'

She did not move, and I, eager to renew my life and my joy in the deep wells of her eyes, spoke again, hoping to make her turn to me. 'You must know why I have brought you here,' I faltered. 'It seems all so strange and so beautiful.'

'Yes, so beautiful,' she echoed.

'Why . . . I don't even know your name,' I murmured, 'but I know that I desperately love you. And you know, too.'

'And yet,' she said, and I could see the tremulous flutter of her bosom, 'and yet I am a stranger to you.'

She moved, ever so slightly. Though still half-turned away from me, her little hand repeated its former gesture of intimate tenderness. I seized it in my own; my tongue was loosed; and I told her my love in language that I had never used in all my life before, save in my secret thoughts. She did not reply when my pleading ceased ; and, bitterly though I longed for her responding vows, I read into her silence a meaning more profound than that of any speech. I with my stammered boyish words, she with her rich silence, had made audible the music of perfected love to which the whole creation moves. She was the incarnate word for which I had dumbly sought. She was the rose of my heart visibly blossoming. She was a dark flame in which I longed to be consumed and re-created.

Still she did not respond. Her hand did not return my pressure. It lay in mine curiously lifeless. A nameless fear set a chill finger upon me. Gently I released her, stood a moment irresolute, and then, with a swift resurgence of passion, I gathered her into my arms. She stood with her back towards me, her head averted. My desirous hands, moving under her arms to caress her breasts, urged her gently backwards towards me. Her head fell upon my shoulder, and my lips sought hers.

Still she did not answer my passion. Her red mouth was dry and harsh against mine : dry, harsh, unresponsive. I drew back, still holding her, and stared in anguish and bewilderment. And what the insane savour of that kiss had hinted to me my naked sight incredibly confirmed. She did not reciprocate my burning desire ; the body that I held was inert, unyielding ; the eyes that seemed to gaze at me were glassy with indifference ; and the face I looked upon, under the merciless moonlight, was a face of painted rag.

4

Pilgrim in an alien world, a world of tangible unreality ; dupe of desire, doomed to the dark house of my solitude ; and now cheated for ever of the beneficent illusion called love ! I do not know for how long after that hellish apocalypse events moved for me in a kind of evil dream, nor how long my tortured spirit hovered on the verge of madness. Perhaps for five seconds, perhaps for twenty, I remained clutching that bundle of clothes. Then, screaming, I flung it from me. With mincing gait it walked away in the direction of the house. I shut my insulted eyes, and a storm of sobbing caught and shook me with fury. A voice at my elbow said : ' Supper is served, sir, if I may take the liberty.' And I looked up to see Dolphin, rubbing his hands together in an ecstasy of deference, and leering like Pandarus. Before I could find a voice for my loathing, he was gone out of earshot.

Had it not been for the thought of Eve,

alone in that house, I could never have endured to return there. But her need was imperative, and an hour later found me huddled and shuddering in the darkness of my bedroom. I sat on my bed, waiting and listening for I knew not what, and still dazed with horror and only half-apprehending the nature of my experience. A hundred explanations visited my distraught mind, all of them monstrous and improbable, but none more monstrous than what my own eyes had seen. The one straw of certainty to which I fiercely clung, with the desperation of a man who feels his reason toppling, was that Dolphin, whether man or fiend, was the presiding genius in this sinister buffoonery. The bed creaked under me whenever I shifted my position. The room was bitterly cold. Once I thought I heard from the room below the sound of men laughing together ; and presently there reached me the regular footfall of some one walking to and fro. I pictured, with shuddering distaste, that long, low, dim-lit chamber, with one figure of mockery, a miracle of mad artifice, pacing it from end to end with sly mechanical smile.

And while, against my will, I listened to this sound, there arose a low wailing, like that of a half-human voice. It increased in volume ; died away ; and then, after a profound pause, returned with greater violence. At first I hardly knew, as gust followed gust, whether it was I or the wind that uttered these starved and animal cries, whether it was the wind or my own insulted spirit that growled round the house and lashed the window-panes with passionate, invisible hands. The storm, within me and without, seized and shook me and flung me sobbing on the bed. I could scarcely distinguish between the rattle of the windows and the chattering frenzy of my teeth ; the shock and boom, as wave after wave of angry air struck the house, was hardly louder than my own heart's clamour. With my face buried in the pillow I saw the stars go giddily up and down the sky, heard great engines throbbing, and felt, or seemed to feel, the house itself tossing and plunging in a waste of furious waters. Mountains of foam, piled round the bleak horizon, rose high and higher, till the sky itself was shut out ; they bore down upon me thunderously, like galloping horses. I held my breath, waiting to be struck and trampled down. At every fresh assault I held my breath ; but each time the wind, having rattled the house, passed harmlessly over it to spend its force in the emptiness beyond. I prayed for silence, and when at length silence came, I prayed again for some trivial sound that should distract me from my thoughts. Exhausted, as by battle, I went to the window and looked out. The wind whimpered and moaned, but in the darkness I could discern no sign of the storm's ravages. I had lived during those few hours a lifetime's agony. I felt limp and weak and desperately alone, yet in some degree cleansed of the poison that had tainted my mind. Horror had half-spent itself in the cries that I had uttered when, face downward on my bed, I had joined my voice to that of the inarticulate element.

I sat down again, thinking desirously of sleep. The cold air seemed to bite into my very bones. A near sound set me listening again in an agony. Steps approached my door. They stopped abruptly; some one tapped, timidly at first, then with more decision.

A girl's voice spoke: 'Mr Pendelling!'

It sounded like Eve Richardson, but voices could be simulated. I did not reply.

'Mr Pendelling! Guy! Are you ill?'

I smiled to myself in the darkness. 'Go away, Master Dolphin! Go away, my fine fellow!'

'It's not Dolphin. Surely you know my voice. It's me. Eve. Eve Richardson.'

I rose from my seat on the bed, and, having lit two candles, approached the door. 'Now listen,' I said. 'If I open the door to you and you are Dolphin, I shall choke you with my naked hands.'

I unlocked the door and flung it open. There stood Eve with frightened eyes. 'Come in,' I said dully, and she fell into my arms.

By the time I had helped her into the room she had recovered her self-possession. She sank into a chair, and stared at me. 'Tell me what has happened. I am frightened.' And when I had told her she clutched at my two hands, and hid her face from me. I raised her to her feet, and obeying our common instinct we soberly embraced. In the warm humanity of that encounter my life was renewed, my cold heart kindled.

'Now you must try to sleep,' she said, with a wise smile. 'To-morrow you will go away, I suppose?'

'Yes. But I can't leave you here alone. I will take you back to your father.'

'Yes, to my father,' she said, moving to the door. 'Good night.'

Left to myself, with no human voice to comfort me, I relapsed once more into brooding horror. One of my two candles was already threatening to burn out, and the other, of which there was but two inches, could not last the night through. In my first reaction from the light in whose beams I had seen that vision of outrage I had hungered for darkness, even for the darkness of the tomb. But now, with equal hunger, I yearned for light. The prospect of enduring a black night's solitude, haunted by hideous memories, broke down my fortitude. I felt as forlorn as a lost child. And Eve, I thought suddenly, perhaps she, too, in her bedroom not five yards distant . . . ?

I stepped into the corridor and softly called to her. There was no response, and I returned to my room and shut myself in again, disappointed. Presently, there came another tapping. Without hesitation I opened the door once more.

Eve stood in the doorway, clad in her dressing-gown.

'Did you call?' she said.

'Eve!' I cried impulsively, unexpected emotion flooding my heart with sudden power. 'Eve, you are alive. I want you.'

'Here I am,' she answered.

'Will you come in?' Misgiving fell upon me. Scrupling to touch even so much as her hand, I stepped aside to let her pass.

'Lock the door,' she said, and stood regarding me with her great eyes. 'Why did you call me?'

'Eve, I'm afraid. I'm childishly afraid to be alone with this dark night.'

She nodded gravely. 'So am I.'

'Then why not stay with me?' I urged. 'You will be, you know, quite safe here.' I blushed for the ineptitude of that assurance.

At that she smiled rather piteously, holding out her hands for me to take. 'Do you think I want to be safe?' she whispered, generously scornful. 'Won't you kiss me again, Guy?'

We had already exchanged the kiss of comradeship. But now, as I held her in my arms, I knew her to be infinitely desirable. My lying heart told me that it was she I had loved from the first. The broad fair brow, the blithe dimpling cheeks, the speaking kindliness of eyes bluer than heaven : these I had often admired, but never with the least pulse of this overmastering emotion. Her face, framed against the mass of dark hair that fell about her shoulders, took on for me suddenly an eternal aspect. This was the face of ideal womanhood, ancient and everlastingly young, this the immortal vision of the world's desire. Passion was in it, and the promise of passion; faith, motherhood, and sublime surrender. 'Eve, lovely Eve, I want you!' Her lips were marvellously vital ; her breath was eager; the smell of her hair intoxicated me. The virginal fire of her eyes, the ardour of her ripe youth, burned away all lingering memory of the day's shame. Life herself was in my arms, ardent-eyed, sweet and lusty of limb, desired and desirous. Upon that mingling of flesh and spirit there could obtrude no thought of a mockery that was worse than death.

5

Not till grey dawn woke us did I recall the horror, and what it might portend. We had arranged, Eve and I, to slip away from the house early, and get a train to London, where in due time we should marry each other. There could be no thought of parting. Eve had quarrelled with her father, had left home, in defiance of his wishes, solely in order to protect me by her presence from the nameless peril that she believed this house held. We put our plans into effect without difficulty, reaching the railway station an hour and a half after we set out. Anxiety, none the less, had taken its toll of our spirits. We had a carriage to ourselves, but we did not care to talk. Already I was beginning to ask myself: Who is this strange young woman?

'Tired?' she asked me, with a sudden shrewd glance at my gloomy face.

'A little. Aren't you?'

THE DARK HOUSE

She did not answer my question. 'Are you sorry about . . . about us ? '

'Not sorry,' I told her. 'Never sorry. But I'm puzzled. Who are you ? How can I ever know you, reach you—you or anyone ? How am I to know that you are not merely another of my . . . inventions ? '

It was a foolish speech. I might have known that she would not understand it. She smiled with infinite tenderness, radiant in her beautiful illusion. But tears stood in her eyes, and she did not answer.

PRENTICE

PRENTICE

ONE is always running across them, these survivors of the dark age. They serve to remind one of the incredible fact that the war really did happen. It was in a public-house not too remote from Fleet Street that I met Jimmy Prentice again, all that was left of him. From his dark corner he stood eyeing me speculatively over the rim of his glass. He lacked an arm; and the livid scar that ran diagonally across his face, breaking the nose in two, lent him a sinister appearance. It was small wonder that I did not at first recognise him, and small wonder that as soon as I recalled his name there flashed into my mind a vision of George Leek. My last sight of Prentice had been at a Casualty Clearing Station behind Vimy. Then, his face had been swathed in bandages, his eyes shaded, his tortured body strapped to a bed. A whole man feels awkward in the presence of such disaster. What could one offer by way of consolation to a man permanently disfigured and disabled? Jimmy Prentice had no more than his share of vanity : that I knew well enough. But, when all is said, many of us would rather lose a limb than have our likeness destroyed. Disablement is disablement, and there's an end of it ; but the face, be it plain or handsome, is one's very self, the living and outward sign of whatever lurks within, and its disfigurement involves, in some sense, a loss of identity. Prentice, therefore, was the victim of a double outrage ; and I was frankly afraid to learn how he was taking it.

'Here's a pal come to see you,' said the medical orderly. To me he whispered : 'Only two minutes.'

'Well, Jimmy,' said I, taking the plunge, 'you've got a Blighty one this time, old cock.'

For a few seconds he made no answer. Seeing his lips move, I bent over him.

'Who's there?' said the grey lips.

I told him my name. 'You remember me, don't you?'

He grunted assent. 'Bit dizzy, that's all. Yes, corp, I got a plateful all right. But nothing to what old George got. Old George Leek.'

This was a dangerous subject. Prentice

and Leek had been inseparable friends ever since I had known them. They came from the same street in Camberwell, but had never met there : a circumstance that not only drew them together but provided them with an inexhaustible subject for conversation and debate. They were for ever delightedly comparing notes about music-halls and cinemas they had both frequented and 'tarts' they had both known ; and it seemed to them marvellous that with all they had in common they might never have become acquainted but for the war. ' Spose you never come across a feller called Spink, George ? 'Im what used to keep a lil paper-shop down the 'Igh Street ? What, you knew 'im ! Fency that now ! You knew old Spink ! ' It seemed too good to be true that Leek had actually bought cigarettes from old Spink. To the bond of these common memories, which gave to Prentice and Leek an illusive grasp upon our vanished civilisation, there was added, during the long alternation of action and so-called rest, the bond of incessant companionship. In the Rest Camp they pooled their wits against the Sergeant-Major, shamelessly dodging fatigues whenever they could ; in the trenches they generally contrived to occupy the same dug-out. Once,

once only, they went over the top together ; more than once, squatting side by side, a shirt spread over each lap, they competed in the slaughter of lice. In this kind of tournament Prentice was generally the victor, though Leek ran him close enough to give a zest to the betting. They were an oddly assorted pair, and there was something correspondingly odd in their relationship. Prentice was— and is—a small, wiry fellow, whereas Leek had a biggish, clumsy body and a red moon face. Through Leek's composition ran a streak of singular simplicity, and, from the very first, little Prentice stood to him in loco parentis. Prentice, in fine, mothered Leek, as one might mother an awkward schoolboy : cheered him when he was down, steered him when he was drunk, and from motives purely sanitary kept him away from brothels. All this, whether at first or second hand, was common knowledge in the platoon ; and it provided me with a good reason for wishing to discourage further mention of Leek. Jimmy Prentice had lost more than a friend : he had lost his child.

'George caught it a lot worse than me,' murmured the man on the bed, and seemed to wait for my comment.

'I know,' said I. 'But your own little

packet'll see you home, Jimmy, well out of this. That's what you've got to think of.'

'Yes, I'm fixed up for duration. Not arf I ain't.' There was curiously little tone in his words. 'I'm a lucky one, corp, there's not a doubt of it. But old George Leek—you oughter seen old George and what they done to 'im, corp. You ought, struth!'

In point of fact I had seen George Leek, and was busy trying to forget the sight. It had confirmed me in the belief that war is an untidy method of settling differences of opinion. I felt a tide of sickness rising in me again, and so, remembering the orderly's injunction, hastened to make my farewells.

'Well, good luck, Jimmy. You'll be back in Camberwell soon, you know.'

It was a stupid blunder, as I realised the moment it had passed my lips. I could not shake hands with him; I dared not so much as lay a finger upon that immobile mass of pain. A touch, had it been possible, would have expressed more for me than my feeble speech, and I was exasperated to be denied it. Yet I was glad his eyes were masked when he said, still without tone, 'No more Camberwell for old George.'

2

These were the memories that stirred in my subconsciousness the other day when I caught sight of Jimmy Prentice flashing mute questions at me over his glass of bitter. I walked over to where he stood.

'I'm sure we've met before. Was it in France?'

'Shouldn't wonder,' he said, with a crooked grin. 'Prentice, my name, sir.'

'Of course!' I remembered everything. 'And mine——'

'Oh, I know *you* right enough,' said Prentice, more at his ease. 'I been lookin' at you this last *ten* minutes.'

'Let's go and sit down—over there,' I said. 'We can talk in comfort.'

We began drinking together and talking over old times. It was not at first very easy going. He began by being cursedly deferential, till I almost wished for another war that should get us back on the old, easy terms. But soon he thawed: told me what pension he got in consideration of his lost arm, and wondered whether the government would consent to take the other at the same price. My own contributions to the talk were somewhat halting, because I could not get the idea of George Leek out of my head and yet was afraid to introduce him into the conversation. This obsession must have made me appear absent-minded, and the consciousness of appearing so added to my embarrassment.

Over his fourth glass Prentice grew pensive. 'I spose,' he said suddenly, 'you wouldn't remember that chap Leek I used to knock about wiv : fat sort of feller wiv a red face ? '

'I remember him very well. He got knocked out in the same scrap, didn't he ? '

'The same strarf,' corrected Prentice. 'Crawling round on your belly and holding what Jerry sent over. Not much scrap about it. Georgie Leek, he was a fair knock-out for getting into trouble. You din know 'im well, did you, corp ? Not to *say* well ? '

'Only by sight,' I admitted. 'I know you two were always together.'

'You've got it,' Prentice assured me. 'Always together we were. And need be, what's more. Would you believe it, 'e come from the same street as me, did George Leek, and we never knew nuffin of it till we got out there. There was suthin about George I couldn't 'elp liking. 'E was like a blessed infant in some ways, though never what you'd call a fool, if you get me. And yet

I dunno. One day 'e dragged me up out of a shell-'ole in the middle of a big straaf, and you'd never guess what for. "Ello, Jimmy," he 'ollers down to me, "you missin' a good thing down there, matey. Jest you kim up 'ere a minute." Course, I tell 'im to go to 'ell, but in the end I 'ad to go up so as to make 'im take care of 'isself. "Now you jest listen," says George, cocking 'is 'ead a one side very sentimental. "Why don't you take cover?" I asks him, mild as milk but the least bit sarcastic. "I've 'eard that ullyballoo before to-day." But there wasn't no arguing wiv George. "No," says 'e. "I din mean listen to Jerry. We've all 'eard *'im*. Listen agin." Then I 'eard what 'e mean—right up in the sky there was a bleedn lil skylark singing like one o'clock. It made me feel queer, but I din let on to George. "Come to that, I've 'eard *that* before," I tells 'im, pretty short. So I had, too, moren once. But that was George all over. He was soft, there's no getting away from it. Did 'e ever tell you about 'is girl Ada?'

I shook my head, and Prentice launched at once into a long and highly circumstantial account of George's girl Ada. George had carried in his wallet six or seven photographs of Ada; and Ada was nominated as sole

beneficiary in the last Will and Testament
that George had laboriously scrawled in the
back of his paybook. Prentice could not deny
that she was a pretty piece, but he would
have it that she was not the girl for George.
George, a hopeless romantic, was very much
in love ; and Ada, it appeared, had neither
difficulty nor compunction in playing ducks
and drakes with him. It was George's trouble,
Prentice told me, that he had never had
anyone to look after him properly, and him
a chap that needed more looking after than
most. His own mother, for example, was
nothing but an Oly Terror. Poor George
had conceived the first and last passion of
his life when he was a mere warehouse lad
with I don't know how few shillings a week.
Even that meagre wage, whatever it was, was
pitilessly seized by his mother, and George
provided with a minute fraction of it for his
daily expenses, so that he was quite unable
to pay Ada those little delicate attentions—
cinemas and fish suppers—that courtship
demands. But the time came when he got
promotion, accompanied by an increase in
salary of sixpence a week. This good fortune
he determined to conceal from his mother.
Thereafter, for ten consecutive weeks, he
secreted a sixpenny piece in the tail of his

shirt. Then he made an appointment with Ada. For that great occasion, said Prentice, George got himself up regardless. He even went so far as to change into a clean shirt. Ada's disgust, when he confessed to having left his money behind, can be imagined, though I gathered from Prentice that she did not put George to the trouble of imagining it. The lover crawled home with his tail between his legs, and faced the second dose of music as best he could. By the fire stood his mother, a picture of wrath. On the mantelpiece, as his guilty eyes were quick to see, was a neat little pile of sixpences. 'Come 'ere, yer cunning little bastard!' cried mother. 'Well, mum,' retorted George, with more spirit than one would have given him credit for. '*You* ought to know.'

'And then,' said Prentice, 'she clouted 'im—a feller, mind you, what could have squeezed 'er silly 'ead off wiv 'is finger and fumb. I'd like to catch *my* muvver at sech tricks. But that,' added Prentice, lapsing into his refrain, 'that was old George all over, soft, soft as pap. As for that Ada, she was a dirty bit of goods and no mistake. Cadgin' and crawlin' and naggin' 'im all in once. Spendin' 'is rhino, and orf wiv other chaps the same day. And did 'e ever learn better? Not 'im. You dunno George if you think 'e learned better, corp. Leaf after leaf he wasted runnin' round after that Ada, the lil bitch ; and if ever he got so much as arf an hour's 'and-'olding on the top of a bus 'e thought isself lucky. The things 'e used to tell me! "You're a good boy, George," she'd say to 'im, laughing up 'er sleeve at 'im or my name's not James Prentice ; "there's no one I'd trust like I trust you, George." 'E din know the first word about wimmin, and that's a fact, corp. Used to make me fair mad to 'ear 'im. She trusted 'im, did she! When he tell me that I jest up and tell *'im* suthin. I tell 'im what she was and what would do 'er good, and, bleeve me or bleeve me not, 'e wouldn't speak to me for a couple of days. Still, I din take offence. Can't take offence wiv a soft bloke like that. Some one got to look after 'im, and me being from the same street, well, I took the job on, any old 'ow. Cleaned 'is buttons and 'elped 'im wiv 'is clobber when we was in barracks, and made 'im keep 'is 'ead down when we wasn't. And I 'ad to be sharp sometimes. 'Ad to pretend I thought the world of 'is girl Ada. When 'e got blotto down at a Base Camp this talk of Ada was the on'y thing ud keep 'im out of mischief. Course

I got a bit short wiv 'im time and agin. I was sorry arterwards. "Your girl Ada," I tell 'im once, "she'll be the deaf of me, George, and of you too, shouldn't wonder." That's what I told 'im, corp, and I wasn't far out—about 'im, any'ow.'

Our glasses stood empty before us on the little round table at which we sat. Prentice declared that he had had enough. He refused my invitation to lunch, but agreed that a snack from the counter would do us both good. When I returned with a plate of sandwiches I asked him to explain in what sense Ada had been the death of George Leek. Whereupon he promptly withdrew his remark. He admitted generously that Ada couldn't help it, poor girl. If George chose to be such a noodle, well, it wasn't really her lookout. What he had meant was that if George hadn't been so soft about that girl, he might never have gone back to get them field-glasses.

'What field-glasses?' I asked. 'This is the first I've heard of them.'

It was, said Prentice, like this here. The company, as I very well knew and no one better, had been holding a very exposed part of the front line. The relief was due in an hour and a half, but the enemy had got our position perfectly sighted and were sending over the best they had got. Their best proved very good indeed. When one in every ten of us had been suitably mutilated the order came through that we were to abandon the position. Its importance, we were led to understand, had been exaggerated, and the men that were to relieve us had been sent elsewhere. The retirement was orderly but hurried, and in the hurry George Leek left behind him a pair of field-glasses entrusted to his care by O.C. Lewis Guns.

'Blimey,' said Leek, 'I'm going back for them, Jimmy.'

Prentice, who was slightly wounded, contented himself with a volley of oaths in disparagement of this suggestion. To carry it into effect involved crawling five hundred yards on one's belly into a shell-swept area.

'And me wallet too,' said Leek. 'I've left me wallet behind, paybook and all.'

At this Prentice took alarm. He knew, as well as Prentice did, what was in that wallet. 'Nah, George,' he said urgently. 'Stay where y'are, boy. No gal's worf it, let alone 'er photer.'

But the ineffable George was already on his way. A few minutes later they heard, even above the shriek of artillery, a devastating human scream.

3

Prentice paused in his narration and stared for several seconds at the dregs in his glass.

He said presently : ' Course I oughta stopped 'im. But I wasn't quick enough, that's all about it, and I'd caught a lil packet in me thigh, what's more. Any'ow, when we 'eard that scream we 'ad to go and see about it. So me and another bloke—Evans, they called 'im—started orf. Oh yes, we got there all right. And we seen George Leek, not arf we didn't. Tell you straight, I never seen sech a sight. 'Ow 'e could scream at all wiv arf 'is face gorn beats me. But scream 'e did and never stopped a moment cep to get 'is breaf back. Lyin' on 'is back all knocked to pieces, 'e was. Tell you straight, corp, I din like it. " Come on, Evans," says I. " We got to get 'im out o' this." So Evans takes 'old of 'is 'ead, and me 'is legs, and— Gawstruf, they twisted all ways! Then George, old George Leek, 'e opened 'is eyes and seen me lookin' at 'im. And suddenly 'e stop 'is row and jest stared up at me. Looked at me sorta sick, as though I'd 'it 'im. Then 'is mouf moved, and 'e said, straight to me, wiv a sort of whistle in his voice, and a sorta sob : " Jimmy . . . Crysake do us in ! "

Well, it was a fair knock-out. I dunno what to do. 'Im all to pieces like that and still alive. No getting 'im back. And whizz-bangs all round us—merry 'ell.'

Prentice's voice wavered and was silent. I did not dare to look up, but presently I asked : 'And what did you do ?'

'Well,' said Prentice, slightly surprised by the question. 'What could I do ? " Cry-sake do us in ! " says old George. So I out wiv me jack-knife and cut 'is bloody froat. 'E was a good pal to me.'

The clock struck. It was three. The barman, who had already uttered several times his warning chant, ' Time, gentlemen, please ! ' now came to reinforce his persuasions. Prentice, before yielding up his glass, drank off the muddy dregs that from time to time during his narrative he had so sadly scrutinised. We got up and sauntered into the street, where, facing each other for a parting word or two, we heard the tavern key turn against us.